Praise for

A LONG WAY FROM DOUALA

"In this artfully constructed and absorbing fiction, Lobe sketches in the multiple tensions in modern-day Cameroon around power, status, religion and regional identity . . . Lobe shows how, in their different ways, the Christian evangelism of the south and the Islamic radicalism of the north both feed off feelings of despair and dispossession. However, the characters in these pages are anything but passive victims, mutinously alive, irreverent, engaged and challenging. Choupi's awareness of his gradual sexual attraction to Simon is beautifully paced, and Lobe is particularly adept at capturing the shift from the lingering pieties of childhood to the abrasive truths of wider, adult worlds . . . Lobe has the ability to summon up whole worlds in a careful economy of phrase, bringing individuals and communities to life beyond the photogenic opportunism of breaking news."

—*Irish Times*, Best New Books in Translation

"Max Lobe has emerged as a name to watch in contemporary Swiss literature . . . the Cameroon-born author has notched up six books and won multiple prizes for his topical, rip-roaring explorations of life, society and politics in both his birth and adopted countries. *A Long Way from Douala* is his fifth novel, and the first to appear in English courtesy of Ros Schwartz's superb translation . . . There's a lot to like about his straight-talking prose and sparky, Camfranglais-sprinkled dialogues, and I'd happily have stayed on board for longer."

—*European Literature Network*

"Max Lobe is a brilliant young talent . . . This defiant and up-lifting immigrant's story is powerful and persuasive . . . [a] stylish and colorful tale, rich and insightful."

—*NB Magazine*

"The stretching Cameroonian roads take on a character of their own. Max Lobe's style is direct, sensual and wholly unique."

—*Afrique Magazine*

"Lobe's poignant tale weaves into a bustling Cameroonian tapestry and explores the complexity of family relationships, love, identity and dreams. We understand why some people run away from home and why they may never look back."

—Yejide Kilanko, author of *A Good Name*

"*A Long Way from Douala* is a lovingly told story about friendship and self-discovery. This brilliant book chronicles two Cameroonian boys from a relatively sheltered upbringing coming of age through an intimate encounter with the diverse worlds and complex characters that make up the Cameroonian experience."

—Ainehi Edoro-Glines, Assistant Professor, University of Wisconsin-Madison

"*A Long Way from Douala* presents readers with nuances of contemporary Cameroon in an age of social media where competing motives related to religion, sport (football) and familial dynamics shift our expectations of the coming-of-age novel. Enlightening for its function as a domestic travel narrative as well as a political survey of the terrorist threats of Boko Haram, the novel reorients us to the meaning of brotherhood and to what drives young people toward migration to Europe. The novel is like a new folklore with

updated riddles to challenge us to decipher the best course of action along life's journey and its crossroads."
—Christel N. Temple, Professor of Africana Studies, University of Pittsburgh

"Redolent with the sights, sounds and smells of modern Cameroon, this is in fact a classic road trip, a Homeric quest in which our two young heroes may not discover what they were seeking but learn a great deal about themselves, each other and the state of Africa. A jostling, poignant tale, it left me hungry for more."   —Michela Wrong, author *Borderlines* and *It's Our Turn to Eat*

"[Max Lobe's] eye is as compassionate as his characterizations are rich. I only wish this novel had been twice the length. You are in for a treat."
—Patrick Gale, author of *Take Nothing With You*

"Max Lobe writes about danger and uncertainty with unwavering compassion and hope. *A Long Way from Doula*— a coming-of-age road trip bursting with love and humor— traces the delicate bonds between parent and child, childhood and adulthood, life and death."
—Catherine Lacey, author of *Pew*

"Max Lobe's *A Long Way from Douala* hits all the sweet spots of a road-trip book: a cast of wild travelers, hurdle after hurdle, and some boneshakingly funny moments. Even with the presence of Boko Haram looming, which adds a frightful dimension, the book never loses its tenderness. I was rooting hard for Jean and Simon."
—Ayesha Harruna Attah, author of *The Hundred Wells of Salaga*

A LONG WAY FROM DOUALA

MAX LOBE

Translated from the French by
Ros Schwartz

Other Press
New York

Production editor: Yvonne E. Cárdenas

10 9 8 7 6 5 4 3 2 1

Library of Congress Cataloging-in-Publication Data
Names: Lobe, Max, 1986- author. | Schwartz, Ros, translator.
Title: A long way from Douala / Max Lobe ; translated by Ros Schwartz.
Description: London ; New York : Small Axes, 2021. | "First published as
Loin de Douala, © Éditions Zoé 2018—Title page verso.
Identifiers: LCCN 2021002000 (print) | LCCN 2021002001 (ebook) |
ISBN 9781635421743 (paperback) | ISBN 9781635421750 (ebook)
Subjects: LCSH: Boko Haram--Fiction. | Sexual orientation—Fiction. |
Cameroon—Fiction. | Cameroon—Description and travel—
Fiction. | Cameroon—Social conditions—Fiction.
Classification: LCC PQ2712.O22 L6513 2021 (print) |
LCC PQ2712.O22 (ebook) | DDC 843/.92—dc23
LC record available at https://lccn.loc.gov/2021002000
LC ebook record available at https://lccn.loc.gov/2021002001

Publisher's Note

For my mother, Chandèze

Translator's Note

Camfranglais is a hybrid language spoken in the Republic of Cameroon where English, French and some 250 indigenous languages coexist. A slang spoken by secondary school students and urban youth, it consists of a mixture of French, English, Pidgin and borrowings from local languages. Camfranglais expressions are italicized the first time they appear and are explained more fully in the Glossary, which begins on page 185.

English words that are italicized in the text indicate that the English word is part of the Camfranglais vocabulary used in the original French.

A LONG WAY
FROM DOUALA

1

It's a February evening in 2014 at the height of the dry season. Even the flies are too exhausted to buzz. They spiral around for a few seconds and then stop.

Soon it will be midnight in Bonamoussadi, a residential neighborhood to the north of Douala. Around the Bijou bakery, a few blocks from our house, bars are closing with a clatter of chains and padlocks. Drunkards bleat for one last beer: "Otherwise we'll sma-sma-smash up this place!" The women bar owners shriek with laughter and send them packing: "Off with you! Out of here, you drunken fools!" Their laughter sounds like a wailing police siren. A hundred meters away, on the main street, the popular Empereur Bokassa bar pounds out the season's hits. You can hear the distant concert of croaking and the mewing of stray cats.

Meanwhile, I'm glued to my desk, revising for my first-year university exams. The bedroom walls are plastered with posters of football champions: my brother Roger's idols. I only recognize the photo of our national team and the one of the legendary Roger Milla. A few aluminium trophies, some cheap medals and countless sports shirts that my brother can't be bothered to put away. His boots stink.

Our bunk bed is opposite the desk. It's more and more cramped for our growing bodies. Roger's asleep on the top bunk, worn out from his secret training sessions. My mind keeps wandering from my books and I gaze fondly at his angular face. I can see Pa in him. They have the same high forehead, hollow cheeks and pointed chin. He's snoring. I can see his dreams of football stardom dissolving in the saliva dribbling from his open mouth. I feel sorry for him and wish that Pa and Ma would stop forcing him down a path that's not right for him. He was born for football. He often tells me excitedly, his eyes shining, "You'll see, little bro! I'm going to make it big! My transfers will cost millions. They'll want me to do trainer ads. Adidas, bro! Adidas! I'll end up on the cover of *Paris Match*. Just you wait! Just you wait!"

Suddenly, Ma's voice hysterical from the next bedroom: "Claude! No Claude, you can't do this to me! No! Get up right now! Get up and walk, in the name of the Lord Jesus!"

Roger's eyes snap open: "Did you hear that?"

As one, we rush in to find Pa lying on the bed. His breathing is very shallow. Hard to know whether he can even still feel his legs. He's barely moving. Part of his face is paralyzed. His left eye's shrunken and closed, and the other one's bulging. His mouth's all lopsided and only opens on the right side.

Pa is unrecognizable.

Muttering a string of prayers, Ma's massaging him with her precious Puget olive oil imported from France.

Oh Lord! Why not get him straight to hospital? No, no. Ma believes in the all-powerfulness of Yésu Cristo! Despite Pa's aversion to the unction, which she paid dearly to have blessed by Pastor Njoh Solo of the True Gospel Church, here she is pouring long, long streams over his cheeks, his shoulders, his whole body. Dousing him all over. She even tries to get him to drink some, but it's no use. Everything that goes into his mouth comes straight out again. Ma's distraught. Has her God abandoned her? Impossible! That's not His way. Maybe the old man can't swallow because it's olive oil, she tells herself. So she runs to fill a glass with water. The water Pa brings home in vast quantities from the SABC, the Cameroon national brewery where he works. Ma had a few liters blessed by the pastor. Convinced that witches were against her marriage, she says it was to ward off evil spirits. But Pa isn't able to swallow that water either.

So Roger fetches some beer, goes over to Pa and raises him up slightly. Our father's bulging eye twinkles at the first drop. He seems to be smiling. He's like a child whose mother gives him mandarin- or mango-flavored cough linctus. But once again, like with the olive oil and the water, nothing; it doesn't work. The liquid's barely past his lips when it froths out again. The only thing left is the Bible, says Ma: "Oh Lord Almighty, thou who givest life, deliver my husband from death in the name of Jesus Christ!" But the more she invokes Yésu Cristo, the more contorted Pa becomes.

She panics and wails: "Oh Good Lord! What have I done to deserve this? Why do you punish your poor servant like this?" Roger kneels beside Pa while I calm our mother down. At that moment, an ocean lies between my brother and me.

Roger rushes out, slamming the door. Ma screams: "Where do you think you're off to?"

What feels like an eternity later, he reappears with our brother-from-another-mother Simon Moudjonguè. On seeing me still sitting beside Ma, Roger clenches his jaw and beckons Simon to come closer. Simon acknowledges me with a nod. His discreet greeting is a question: "What's the matter *this time*?" Roger takes hold of Pa's right shoulder. Simon helps him. His eyes are shining with resolve. Only his hands are shaking. The two of them carry Pa outside to the waiting taxi.

We're all on edge. Is Pa still alive? Ma keeps yelling: "Where are you taking my husband, Roger?" Then she adds: "Simon! Simon, answer me!"

A few shadowy figures gather under the wan light of the street lamp. The neighbors. Both curious and concerned. Two drunks stagger over to join the knot of women. They yell: "Hey you! You . . . You haven't got a nice, cool little bottle of Cas-Castel, have you?"

Roger's chest frantically rises, falls and rises again. He's sweating, he wipes his forehead. Once inside the taxi, he lays Pa's head in his lap. Simon, in the front, shouts at me: "To the General Hospital!" As it drives off, the car stirs up a great cloud of dust. Ma collapses. The neighbors come and help me support her. One of the drunks clears his throat then hums: "You drink 'am, you die, You don't drink 'am, you still die!" His rasping voice mingles with the croaking and mewing.

And that's how Pa died.

2

Contrary to all expectations, a few months earlier, my brother had gained his school certificate. Granted, it was his fourth attempt. At the same time, I'd passed my baccalaureate, at the age of seventeen, following in the footsteps of Simon, who was already at university.

To celebrate Roger's school certificate and my baccalaureate, our parents threw a big party, to which they'd invited family and neighbors. Our brother-from-another-mother Simon had come from Ngodi-Akwa, across town, to help out. We stacked the crates of beer that Pa brought back from the SABC in the kitchen. Pa capered about like a mountain goat: at last his son had passed his school certificate!

We'd given the sitting room a thorough spring-clean and arranged chairs against the walls to free up a big space in the center. For dancing. The only chair that stood out was Pa's armchair, recognizable both because of its imposing size and the slightly old-fashioned charm of its carvings.

Our local chief, Pa Bomono, and his wife had ringside seats. They wouldn't have missed that party for anything in the world. You should have seen them! They wore their finest traditional costumes. He, a white shirt with a silky black *pagne* tied around his hips. She, a voluminous ankle-length dress with wide sleeves: the *kaba ngondo*. When Pa complimented them on their outfits, the delighted Pa Bomono had replied: "Oh my brother Moussima! In this neighborhood, it's not every day that we see boys of barely seventeen obtain their baccalaureate, is it!" Pa laughed grudgingly while Ma admired Ma Bomono's kaba ngondo. "Thank you. Thank you very much, sister. It's for our son Jean's baccalaureate," Ma Bomono replied, revealing the gap between her teeth.

Everyone was there, even the women my mother described morning, noon and night as witches envious of her marriage. The youngest of them, the *panthers*, wore little clothing. Ma Bomono was shocked: "What is this way of dressing? Anyone would think the market was out of fabric!"

The owner of the Empereur Bokassa had briefly shut the bar. She'd been followed by a few drunkards, desperate for the slightest drop of free alcohol. They'd installed themselves on the porch, near Roger's friends, who were lustily eyeing the panthers' plunging necklines. They talked not of their buddy's school certificate, even less of my baccalaureate, but of their exploits and the upcoming matches of their football team, the Nyanga Guys of Bonamoussadi.

Simon's mother, Sita Bwanga, arrived a little later. She parked her blue Toyota RAV-4 in front of our iron gate and started hooting the way people do on their way to a wedding. Jesus! Anyone would think Cameroon had just won the Africa Cup of Nations. Ma and the other women went out to greet her. You should have seen them dancing, clapping their hands and singing: "*O wassé! O wassé!* Here we come! Here we come!" Sita Bwanga pulled several boxes of champagne out of her car. Moët. "It's to celebrate our son's baccalaureate!" she announced, while the women ululated continuously as they do at bride-price ceremonies.

And Ma yelled: "Where on earth has that lazybones Roger got to? Tell him to come here and carry these boxes!"

My parents had laid on food: banana fritters, fried plantain, a delicious sauce of red beans with palm oil and chicken wings roasted with tomatoes. Raising a spoonful of sauce to his lips, Pa Bomono stained his white shirt. "You'll eat yourself to death!" snapped Ma Bomono, glaring at him. This was met with hearty laughter. Ma turned to Roger: "Can't you see we need a cloth to wipe it off?" I know Pa wanted to speak up in Roger's defense. After all, it was *his* Roger. But how could he? Ma would kill him!

Pa had brought out our entire stock of beer. Simon, Roger and I had the job of serving. We ran to and fro between the kitchen, the living room and the porch. Our hi-fi pumped out old Makossa hits: our parents' favorites. A few women neighbors of their generation, also wearing kaba ngondos, had begun shimmying in the empty space at the center of the room. They looked like they were showing off: you can't dance the Makossa without showing off.

On the porch, meanwhile, the panthers and the football guys were getting all huggy-huggy in a very suggestive way. Luckily they were far from the eyes of the older folk, otherwise Ma Bomono would have given them a piece of her mind.

There were outbursts of laughter, sometimes shrill, sometimes booming. Glasses and plates were knocked over, broken. Roger, Simon and I would rush over to clear up, collect the shards and scraps of food. As we passed, the guests called out to us above the din: "Hey you! *Na how 'na*? Where's my beer? I've been waiting ages! Is it coming or not, jooor?"

Our house had turned into a giant bar.

In the living room, Sita Bwanga was sitting next to Ma. They were whispering in each other's ears like two teenage girls, and they'd burst out laughing throatily, slapping their hands together. *Tos-tas!* Over the general buzz, I heard Sita Bwanga say to my mother: "It's our sons Jean and Simon who are going to *elevate us* in this country." And they hooted again.

Regardless of his state of advanced drunkenness, Pa said to Roger: "Son, mix me my . . . my beer with the palm wine that Pa Bo-Bomono brought." He took a good swig of this mixture then burped: "Ah, my son! Moët, compared with this, I swear it's . . . cat's piss!" and there they were, Pa Bomono, Roger and him, rolling around laughing. What was so funny?

Pa wiped his mouth with the back of his hand. Then, suddenly, he clapped his hands to ask for everyone's attention. "Oh God! What kind of speech was he going to make, in his state? Gradually, a hush fell over the room. Then Pa cleared his throat noisily, thrust out his chest and launched into a tirade punctuated with hiccups and plaudits: "My f-friends, thank you very much for being h-here in such large numbers to celebrate the baccalaureate of my deserving son Jean Moussima Bobé." Applause smothered my surprise. Was it really me he was calling his *deserving son*?

"Truly, I th-thank you on behalf of Roger, too!" More applause and a smile from Ma.

"I am so p-proud of my son Jean. Look what one tiny seed from me has pro- produced. A genius! A NEinstein! A Socrates! And even a Barack Obama!" Bursts of laughter and never-ending ululations.

Ma shot Pa a scornful, annoyed look. Was he trying to highjack me, her star? Besides, hadn't she told the whole of Bonamoussadi and far beyond that I, her Choupinours – her little teddy bear – was gifted? Hadn't she said that her little Choupi had inherited her great brain? Noticing that my mother was looking a bit put out, her bosom-friend Sita Bwanga tapped her on the thigh: "Hey sister! No need to be angry about that, jooor? Men are all the same, you know: when it's good, they say it's all thanks to their seed alone, and when it's bad, it's always our fault. Let him talk his talk-talk as much as he likes. Come on, let's drink our champagne!"

Even though they were already sozzled, the guests cracked open more and even more beers. With their teeth. They clinked bottles, drank straight from the neck then burped loudly. At one point, some of the guests began predicting a golden future, but only for Simon and me. "You, Jean, you'll be the minister of shumthing very important in this country!" a woman neighbor with a shaved head struggled to articulate. "No, no," argued the owner of the Empereur Bokassa from the terrace where she sat. "I'm certain Jean will be an important banker in the United States of America, or in Switzerland, like Simon!" "*Johnny for President!*" barked a drunk. Pa Bomono had a fit of hiccups that made him almost fall off his chair. Then he regained control of himself and breathed deeply. For him, not a doubt: I'd win a Nobel Prize! Whereas Pa hadn't said a word, Ma and Sita Bwanga on the other hand, all emotional, their eyes gazing up at the heavens, repeated: "May the Good Lord hear you! Amen!"

Roger had retreated to the dining room. Stony-faced, he was fiddling with his phone when Simon and I joined him. "But my bro-brother Claude," Pa Bomono said to my father, laughing. "Your seed, eh? You say it produces . . . er . . . that it produces geniuses . . . eh? But you're the only one who thinks that. Because the streets are teeming with beer and football ge-ge-geniuses." Ma and some of the women burst out laughing.

Pa bowed his head. Shame weighed so heavily on his shoulders that he slumped in his chair. This was going too far! He had to say something. He had to put things back in perspective. Dammit!

The young Nyanga Guys of Bonamoussadi hadn't appreciated Pa Bomono's comments either and had made it known by shouting back. Threats to beat him up and curses were traded between them and the old folk. Fingers pointing straight as arrows. A hail of insults. Suddenly, Pa stood up, turned off the music and ordered the guests to leave. "Oh Claude Moussima! We haven't even . . . haven't even begun to celebrate Jean's success and you're already kicking us out? *Na how 'na?*"

"You can go and sleep off your beers in your own homes!"

"Can' even have a li'l laugh here," complained Pa Bomono lurching toward the door, followed closely by his wife.

"Everyone out!"

Even so, some of the neighbors congratulated me one more time: "Well done, Jean! Keep it up, my son!"

The lady with the shaved head spoke to my brother: "Ah Roger! Your turn will come, too. Just ask Jean and Simon to help you, that's all. *Jooor?*"

Roger said nothing. He didn't even look at the people who spoke to him. He ran straight to our room and Simon followed him. But he'd already shut the door. "Open up!" Simon demanded. "Open up, Roger!" No reply. He needed to be alone. Alone with his football kings and his dreams of fame and fortune.

3

The sunlight filtering through the slats burns my eyes. I wake with a jump. I can hear the tweeting of the weaver birds and the first thing I see is my brother Roger sitting in a corner. He's curled up in a tight ball, like a snail that's just been attacked. A big ball. On the wall behind him, the poster of Roger Milla, the great Cameroonian football star of the 1990s. On seeing me, Roger unfolds his arms and raises his head slightly. His hollow cheeks are damp. They glisten in the light. My brother's crying. He's crying so hard his teeth are chattering.

Ma phoned me the day before, shortly after she left for the General Hospital. Through her tears, she announced the news. When I asked her if I could join them, her and Roger, she said: "Oh no, Choupi! You mustn't see this. Stay at home and pray. Pray for your mother. Please, Choupi?" Although shaken, I haven't been able to shed a tear. Not even one tear! I lay in bed for a long time, my eyes open, in disbelief. I don't even know how I eventually managed to fall asleep.

I go over to Roger but not too close either because the look he gives me, oh Lord! – a look filled with pent-up rage, and then the attitude of his hunched body seems to be plotting something explosive, and that stops me from hugging him. I sit down beside him. Calmly, I say: "Are you okay?" No reply, naturally. A long silence occasionally broken by a hiccup or the singing of the birds. He clenches his jaw, his fists, too. From time to time, he blows his nose into his football shirt. He's trembling like a leaf and to me he looks as vulnerable as a child abandoned by its parents in a torrential July downpour. I've never seen him in such a state, not even when Ma beats him black and blue.

I try to place a hand on his shoulder. He pushes it away. On top of Pa's death, he still hasn't got over the unfortunate incident that happened during the party. Since that day, we've barely spoken. He responds to my timid greetings with a threatening look. Since that infamous day, he hasn't spoken a word to anyone in the house, except Pa.

The words, half-formed sentences and speeches I'd like to say to him are stuck inside me. I can't get them out of my belly where they jiggle around and dance the Makossa. But, *I swear*, I want to tell Roger that Pa's death has affected me, too. If I didn't go to the hospital, it was only because Ma made me stay at home. I want to tell him that I understand him; of course I understand his pain, for goodness' sake! Maybe he imagines that now his life will be hell. Contrary to what he thinks, Ma doesn't hate him. I know she doesn't hate him. She beats him, yes, for sure. She gives him thrashings that knock him out for two days, yes. But, deep down, I know she doesn't wish him harm. I want to apologize for Ma, for all the times she beat him. I want to apologize for her obstinate refusal to allow him to go to a professional football academy. Now he's got his school certificate under his belt, who knows, he could ask her again. She might eventually come round. Even if that's very unlikely now Pa's dead.

Most of all I want to say to him: "You know, my very own Roger Milla, I love you so-so much." Exactly that, spoken like that, calmly, clearly, in such a way that he won't doubt my sincerity. But I say nothing. It's not done, that kind of declaration between brothers. At least not like that.

I rub my eyes. The daylight feels harsher than usual. In spite of everything, I'm still not able to cry like Roger. Deep down, I feel, not indifference – that's not it – but a silent unease, and, despite everything, the will to live. Pa's dead, okay, but we still have Ma: life goes on!

Roger probably finds my outward composure surprising, and no doubt shocking. What can I say? . . . The truth is, I'm surprised myself. But there you go, that's how it is: there was never any love lost between Pa and me.

My brother suddenly leaps to his feet, blows his nose, clears his throat and then begins to speak. He finds the words slowly at first, hesitantly, they come to him one by one. He flounders like someone addressing a crowd for the first time. Then his voice becomes louder. And he speaks nonstop – a whole torrent of words. He tells how Pa died very soon after Ma arrived at the General

Hospital. He saw a link between cause and effect. He said: "That woman is a witch! Why didn't she think to take Pa to the hospital sooner? Why did she keep him at home when she could see he wasn't at all well? Why? Can you tell me, you, her adored Choupi? She couldn't even help her husband, that foolish woman! Holy oil, holy water . . . Yeah, that's right! Your God's holy ass, yeah! That woman spent her time wasting all my father's money on that church hocus-pocus with her stupid pastor. So where was your God when it came to saving Pa, then? Where was he?"

When he mentions Ma, his face contorts. His mouth puckers as if he's swallowed a kilo of bitter kola. Disgust, but also accusation. His gestures, the tone and loudness of his voice suggest that it's because of *that* woman that Pa's dead. He says it clearly: "You killed him! You and your *mother*, you killed him!" I don't have time to grasp what he's just said before he adds, with such a serious and contemptuous air: "So, mother's little college boy! You're happy now, aren't you? When the cat's away, the mice will play! Oh, mother's beloved Choupi! Choupi this, Choupi that! That's what you two have always been like in this house. That woman and you, it's always about you, the world revolves around you! You are disgusting egoists! With your Church full of shit, hypocrites and beggars! You're the demons! The vampires!"

I have a cramp in my belly. A lump in my throat. My eyes are wide open, I want to make sure that this is actually Roger talking to me. Of course it's him. He's frothing at the mouth, his chest thrust out in anger. He's shaking and sweating with rage. He points at me: "You, your mother's pious little brainbox, you've always hated me. Oh yes you have! Do you think I don't see your little game with that woman? I know you both hate me. Don't you? You loathe me! Pa's body's still warm and you find the time to sleep. Your mother's clever Choupi-Choupi is nice and snug in his bed, snoring his head off! Oh no, no, no! He's cool, he is! You disrespect Pa's body. You should be ashamed. Ashamed! You and that woman should be ashamed!"

"Ashamed of what?"

I'm surprised by my tone of voice. It's a cross between fear and aggression. My heart is doing the Douala marathon. I don't know how I found the courage to get up. I stand facing Roger. It's as if we're in a cockfighting ring.

"You killed him!" he barks again, pointing at me.

"You're sick. You're completely mad, Roger!"

"This is what I was saying! Look at you, Ma's clever little Choupi-Choupi! Who knows it all. Who's going to save the world! Hallelujah! Hallelujah Choupi!"

"Bah . . . it's not my fault if you're useless."

"What? What did you say?"

"You heard."

I didn't see those two slaps coming. They landed on my face like a rockslide in the season of torrential rains. Stunned, I crouch down to take them; Roger carries on pummeling me. I keep my chin lowered onto my chest to protect my face and put my hands behind my head: that's what Roger does when Ma beats him. I feel the force of his kicks. They're even more powerful than his fists. I've become a punch bag. My ribs hurt. I hear him yelling between gasps: "Dog! Moron! Son of a whore! Choupi-whore, that's you!"

The ordeal lasts a good while.

I can't see his face and he can't see my streaming tears. He's so out of breath that I can hear his heavy, fitful gasping. He clears his throat and spits on me. His hot phlegm slides down my back. "Choupi-whore, that's you!"

A draft of cool air blows in through the window. The birds outside are still cooing. Keeping my head down, I pray that Roger won't hit me anymore. I hear him coming and going around the room. He moves away then returns. He thumps the wall behind me. He yells. He roars like a lion, like a striker after scoring. (I discover later that he's disfigured the picture of Roger Milla.)

After a while, I look up and see a lost man. He is in tears. Does he regret hitting me so hard? Is he wondering what will become of him now Pa's dead and he'll have to survive with *that woman*? His lips are tomato red. His nostrils are quivering. He wipes away a long string of snot with the back of his hand. He clenches his fists. He takes a step toward me, and I quickly bow my head again.

Roger picks up his big sports holdall, strides over to our cupboard and takes out a few things: football shirts, shorts, socks, shin pads, T-shirts, football boots and jeans. He slams the bedroom door. I limp after him: "Where are you going? Roger, where do you think you're going, hmm?" No answer. He comes back, shoving past me. After raiding our parents' room, he leaves. Once again, the squeak of the iron gate opening. And that's it.

I follow him out to the front of the house, then I go back into my room to phone Simon to let him know.

4

In the living room, all the furniture's arranged the same way as for the party to celebrate my baccalaureate and my brother's school certificate. But on this day in early March 2014, the big space in the center of the room will not be for dancing. It's occupied by Pa's coffin.

Nkono, Ma's elderly uncle, a guy with hair that's completely white, has the job of opening the coffin. He does this with all the precautions it requires. Ma lets out a long wail. As one, the women start weeping. They roll on the floor, stamp their feet and yell. Sita Bwanga says that the Heavens snatched Pa from us too soon. Ma Bomono says that he was still so young, so kind. The owner of the Empereur Bokassa holds her by the arm to comfort her.

Pa's body is squeezed into a black three-piece suit that contrasts with his dazzling white shirt. But on his feet, he's wearing only socks, which are also white.

Pa's expression is gentle. Almost smiling. There's cotton wool in his nostrils and ears. His arms are by his sides. He looks so peaceful that I believe he might wake up. "Oh Ngonda! What's happened to my shoes?" he'd ask

Ma. "I'm not going to worship at the mosque." And she'd answer: "Claude, I've already told you a thousand times to stop drinking. And now you've lost your shoes."

I'm struck by the contrast between Pa's tranquility and the women's hysterical weeping. I recall the poem that we used to recite at primary school, "The Breath of Ancestors" by Birago Diop:

> *Those who have died are not gone*
> *They are in the darkness around*
> *The darkness that fades*
> *The dead are not underground*
> *They are in tree that shivers*
> *The woods that quiver*
> *The water that runs loud,*
> *In a hut, in a crowd*
> *The dead are not dead.*

I say these words in my head, over and over like a psalm. My eyes mist over. I don't know why. Is it because Ma's so unhappy? I clench my jaw. No way am I going to cry in front of everyone. Like the women. Me, I want to be like Ma's old uncle, his face serious, composed. Or, possibly, like our neighborhood chief, Pa Bomono: he drinks palm wine to drown his sorrow.

I feel as if I'm seeing Roger in the coffin. An older Roger. That's what he'll look like when he leaves us for good. Because he's already left us. His will be the biggest absence from the ceremony. We've had no news of him since that morning when he beat me up.

Reported missing.

A few days after Pa's funeral, urged by our mothers, Simon and I carried out a preliminary little investigation in the Bonamoussadi neighborhood. One afternoon, we visited the homes of every one of Roger's friends – the footballers he'd invited to the ill-fated party for his school certificate. Nothing. We even went as far as Beedi, our childhood district. Under a merciless sun, we went down all the dusty alleyways of the seedy *sôlô-quarter* in search of Roger's former teammates. Like Jehovah's Witnesses, we went from door to door: houses, small shops – the whole lot. We knocked. We questioned. When necessary, we showed a photo of him posing, smiling, bare-chested, in red shorts with a ball at his feet. Each time, people shook their heads. They all said the same thing: "We haven't seen him since your father passed away. Not even with our own eyes."

Eventually, we ended up back on the main road. Once there, unlike at Pa's funeral, I broke down. I simply couldn't hold back my tears.

In front of Simon, I can cry.

He laid his hand on my shoulder. "We'll find him, don't worry. Calm down. Everything's going to be okay," he said.

A taxi pulled up near us in a cloud of dust. We were about to leave the area we grew up in when Mabingo came over. Simon knows him well. When they were younger, they both played in the football team Roger had got together and of which he was the undisputed captain.

"Hey guys! Are you off without saying hello to your old friend Mabingo?"

"Listen Mabingo," Simon replied, "this is no time for joking. Get it?"

"What? Now who's died?"

"We're looking for Roger. You haven't seen him by any chance?"

Mabingo broke into a mocking laugh.

Simon asked me to go ahead and get into the taxi because the driver was losing patience. "Serious as ever, aren't you Simon?" Mabingo exclaimed. "We can't even have a joke with you."

"Have you seen Roger, yes or no?"

Well yes, he had seen him.

I got out of the taxi to listen. He'd seen Roger a couple of weeks earlier: he was dressed in jeans, ripped at the knees, and a green sports shirt like the one worn by our national football team. (That's what Roger had on the day he ran away.)

"And anyway, you know, don't you Simon, that Roger's not too fond of his mother. That's right, isn't it, Jean?"

"Did he tell you where he was going?" I asked.

"To Europe!" replied Mabingo with a long, cynical laugh. "Yes, guys! Our Roger Milla is *go*, he is, to *Mbeng*! He told me he wanted *boza*: that he was going to walk all the way to Europe. We sold some jewelry. I think it belonged to *that* woman. Isn't that right, Jean? Anyway, guys, he may already be in Nigeria as we speak, la la la! Happily making his way to Spain. Oh, Roger! He's amazing, that guy! Real Madrid, guys! FC Barcelona! Don't they mean anything to you? Doesn't it make you dream? Roger's going to bring us millions and millions! Hey, Jean, don't forget ton-ton Mabingo when your brother's *loaded*, will you?"

"Jean, we're going."

"Hey Simon!" shouted Mabingo. "How come you're off so soon?"

"We're going to look for Roger."

"What about me?"

"What about you?"

"The *news* I just gave you, do you think it's free? Buy me a beer at least for the saliva I've used up."

"Jean, we're going."

5

Boza here has nothing to do with the Turkish drink boza. According to our Cameroonian French dictionary, it's a new word that comes from some West African dialects. Apparently, it means "victory." When people finally set foot on European soil, after months or even years, risking their lives on tortuous routes, they shout: "Boza! Victory!"

Boza means adventure. A complicated journey in small stages that takes the *bozayers* from Cameroon to Europe.

Simon and I try to explain this new vocabulary to our mothers. I'm surprised they've never heard those words. Roger is by no means the first to try his luck at this kind of adventure. Despite the depressing return of the unlucky *bozayers*, nothing dampens the fervor of those setting out. Every day, youngsters decide to attempt boza after having had their visa applications turned down once or twice. The subregional networks are getting organized and are increasingly powerful. Some families break open their piggy bank – years of savings! They pay dearly for a marabout or an evangelist pastor to bless their investment. They hope that the bozayer will quickly find his place among the bright lights of Europe and come back here with pockets bulging. Amen! They keep repeating: "The White man himself says all roads lead to Rome, doesn't he? So let people *choose their road*."

Sita Bwanga is sitting next to her bosom-friend. She holds her hand and strokes it from time to time. Ma is staring at the floor. She is absent. At one point, she wipes her cheeks. Simon, his mother and I are conscious of it.

Silence.

We are at a loss as to how to comfort her.

Since Pa's death, Ma either talks nonstop, or she is silent. There's not one evening when she doesn't cry and ask the Good Lord what she's done to deserve this. Sometimes, from my room, I hear her interminable wailing interspersed with sobs: "Oh Claude!" she moans. "More than twenty years of marriage and this is how you leave me! I told you to control that child. Didn't I tell you? But you didn't listen. You left all the dirty work to me. And now look what's happened! You see! And where are you to take your share of the blame in all this? Where are you, Claude?" She clears her throat and blows her nose, then goes on: "Oh men! Men! If only they'd listen to us once in a while . . ."

I've always known Ma to be strong. She made the decisions and Pa went along with them. He sometimes stood up to her, yes, yes, it did happen occasionally, but, in the end, he'd give in. Ma boasts that her husband was like her bed: she'd trained him so that she could rest on him. She often used to say to him: "I am the tree and you are the bird. Fly off as you please, you will always come back to sit on my branches." Or: "I am the petrol station and you are the car. Drive, drive you fool, go on! In the end you'll be back to guzzle me, jooor." Pa's dead, but she carries on talking to him. Often, she curses him like a kid who's hyper, fired up with hatred and threatening to beat up his classmates. She warns: "In any case, Claude, you and I will fight it out in heaven! I'm telling you!" Strangely certain that she has a place in paradise . . . and that her husband is there already, waiting for her!

Since Pa's death, Ma no longer eats. Flat refusal. No one, not even me, her beloved Choupinours, is able to reason with her. Every day, Sita Bwanga, Ma Bomono, the owner of the Empereur Bokassa and other neighbors bring her full plates of food. *Ndoleh* and boiled cassava, pumpkin-seed cake, braised mackerel, *nsanga*, fried chicken and lots of other dishes. They say: "Come, Sita Moussima, you must eat. Are you going to starve yourself to death before our eyes because of a man who's dead and buried? *Bad luck!*" If only Ma had the ears to listen to them. She doesn't hear them. Like this morning in front of Simon, Sita Bwanga and me, she refuses to speak and keeps her head bowed.

Simon says: "Roger will never have enough money for boza. Even if he sells the jewelry he's taken, even if he does hundreds of odd jobs, he'll still be short. Nor will he have enough to come back if he wants to. We can't just sit here twiddling our thumbs as if everything were fine. We have to do something."

"But what?" asks Sita Bwanga.

Simon scratches his stubble then looks at me. I have nothing to suggest. I swat away two mosquitoes. Simon ends up wondering whether we should contact the police; they can at least put out a missing person appeal with a reward offered. If we trust Mabingo's information – which seems plausible – Roger must be heading for the north, even the far north. It's the route taken by the bozayers to get to Nigeria, the first stage in their bid to reach Europe.

Sita Bwanga is skeptical. She thinks that offering a reward in exchange for information will only result in false sightings. Any self-respecting Cameroonian will do anything to make money out of another's suffering. Isn't it true that one man's loss is another man's gain? She insists we shouldn't drag the police into this business. She says: "Simon, my son! Not the police, whatever we do, no! I am your mother and I know this country better than you do. Okay? How can you trust that corrupt gang who are only interested in a fat envelope? Have you ever heard with your own ears of the police finding a missing person in this country? Have you? We'd have long since heard about it! So, *keep those people well away from the case.*"

While Simon and his mother argue about the merits of going to the police, I watch Ma. What could be going through her head? Is she thinking about the life she's going to have to make for herself now Pa's dead? Since he was an executive at the SABC, we may receive a widow's pension. When he was made deputy brewing manager, we'd already changed our lifestyle. Ma had insisted we move out of the neighborhood. She'd also insisted on a single-family home in Bonamoussadi. She couldn't stand Beedi and its sleazy *sôlô-quarter* anymore. Too overcrowded, too much dust, too many overflowing drains, too many mosquitoes, too many walls with elephant's ears, and most of all . . . most of all, too many witches who wanted her nouveau-riche husband to repudiate her. What is she going to do? Now who's she going to fight against?

The sound of Ma clearing her throat interrupts the argument between Simon and his mother. Immediate silence. Ma looks up, wipes her damp cheeks and gives a drawn-out sigh. We are all ears as she mutters through her sobs: "Go and look for my son. That's all I ask. It doesn't matter what I've done to him, he's still my son. Bring him back here to me. Is that asking too much? Bring him back. That's all I want." Sita Bwanga immediately puts her arms around her. Simon gives me a strange look: "You know, we could go and look for him, you and me."

Taken aback, I look up at him and think almost automatically of the time it would take us. We'd have to decide on a departure point, an arrival point, how we'd go about looking for him and all that stuff. God! Oh Simon! You don't rush headlong into an adventure like that on impulse. And supposing Roger's already managed to reach the African shores of the Mediterranean, supposing he's already aboard a boat?

"Look at your mother," says Simon. "Do you want her to remain in that state? Do you? I'm absolutely certain that Roger hasn't crossed the northern border yet. He must be in Cameroon and we can still find him. I don't know how long we need: a few days, a few weeks or a few months. How should I know? But it's not impossible."

"And who'll stay with Ma in the meantime?" I ask half-heartedly.

"My mother's here. Sita Moussima can come to stay at our place in Ngodi-Akwa until we get back. It will be good for her to get out of this house for a while and go and live somewhere else."

If Simon's suggestion leaves me in any doubt, his eyes convince me. He has irresistible long eyelashes that curl upward. I don't know who he gets his dark, intense gaze from. Perhaps from the father he's never met. In any case, not from his mother, whose eyes are bulging and alarmed.

"If we find him, what do we tell him, hmm?"

"To come home, of course. It's simple, isn't it?"

"What if he doesn't want to?"

"At least we'll have seen him. We'll find out where he is and where he wants to go. I don't know . . . but we have to do something." A few more words, questions, then he announces: "We're leaving in a few days' time."

I don't have much time to find an excuse, a pretext, to get out of this trip. Of course, I want Roger to come back home! But not under any conditions. We're not going to set off in search of him with no pointers, no itinerary and no guarantee of any kind that we'll find some trace of him. Where will we go to inquire about him? The towns? The villages? Which towns? Which villages? Asking around in Beedi or Bonamoussadi is one thing, but embarking on a search for a person throughout the whole of Cameroon . . . Besides, Simon and I have to revise for our upcoming exams. These are my first university tests.

"Simon," I say, looking at my feet to avoid his gaze. "You know we've got exams in a few days."

"That makes no difference. We'll leave right afterward."

"But . . ."

"Are you coming with me, yes or no?"

Ma cries all the time we're talking. Sita Bwanga still has her arms around her and is stroking her back as she would a baby.

6

The living room of the White House in Ngodi-Akwa is on the ground floor. It is maybe two or three times bigger than the one in our single-family house in Bonamoussadi. The floor is covered with eggshell-colored tiles. The walls are painted white and hung with African artworks and photos. One of them is a family photo of Sita Bwanga and her children – Simon and his sister, Kotto. One wall is reserved for Simon's certificates. They are meticulously displayed in gilded wood frames. The ceiling has white plaster moldings. That's the type of material that Ma had asked Pa to put in our house. She wanted to replace our ceiling of varnished plywood with "something much more stylish," she'd say with a sulky expression, then adding: "Something like my sister Bwanga's plasterwork, for instance."

Sita Bwanga is sitting next to Ma, on the black leather sofa. She asks Simon and me if we've got everything we need. We have our smartphones, our chargers – the most important things. We've even ordered two other backup phones and a portable charger. In our backpacks: a New Testament with a blue cover – the Gideon version that also contains the Psalms, our ID cards, some clothes, soap, a toothbrush, toothpaste and disposable Bic razors (only Simon uses them, I don't shave yet). We've packed sandals, a medical kit, two school novels and some paracetamol and Mixagrip flu tablets just in case. We've also got some cash. Just the minimum. You don't want to carry too much on you: thieves have a nose and are never far away. If we run out of money, we can always withdraw some from a cash machine, or our mothers will do a transfer via mobile.

Ma cries when the time comes for us to leave. Loneliness will certainly gnaw at her heart. Of course, her bosom-friend Sita Bwanga will be there to support her and wipe away her tears. But it's not the same. Hugging me tight, Ma says, through her tears: "My little Choupi, Mama's Choupinours, Yésu protect you. May He protect your brother Simon and you on your journey. May everything that the devil puts in your way be destroyed in the almighty name of Yésu Cristo."

"Amen," breathes Sita Bwanga.

"We should go now," says Simon, glancing at his watch. "Our bus leaves in just under an hour."

Simon and I say goodbye, adieu perhaps, to the White House. Our mothers wave us off from the doorway. Sure, Sita Bwanga, with her RAV-4, could have driven us to the Security Voyage bus station in the center of Akwa. But to do so, she'd either have had to leave Ma on her own or bring her along, too. But grief has transformed Ma into a little gray mouse; she won't leave her hole. And so, the two women limited themselves to a cursory goodbye, a hug, a slow hand-wave and a tear or two as they wished the travelers a safe and sound return, adding, their voices quavering: "Take care!"

The minute we set out, I start crying like a *mougou*, a real crybaby. Simon tries to calm me down. It's no use. He asks if I want him to carry my backpack. I shake my head. He looks straight ahead and walks on bravely. He's not like me. Not like a child whose mother has to force him to go to school. He's as courageous as Kirikou preparing to wage war on the sorceress Karaba. But he knows. Oh, he knows why I'm crying!

I'm crying not so much because I'm embarking on a strange adventure with Simon, no, because Simon alone is enough to fascinate me: he's charming, likable, protective . . . He's reassuring. I'm thrilled to be spending these coming days with him. Nor am I crying because I'm leaving Ma behind, either. After all, I no longer suck my thumb. I'm eighteen and I'm at university. Besides, I've already been on holiday on my own to stay with Sita Mpondo, a cousin of Ma's who lives in Olembe, in the north of Yaounde. I'm crying because of a terrible piece of news I've just received.

We were upstairs, in the bedroom, packing our stuff when Simon held out his phone: "Read this."

"What is it?"

"There was another Boko Haram attack yesterday in the north."

"What?"

"But it's not too serious."

The newsflash explains that the Islamist group struck twice in the northern town of Kolofata, close to the border with Nigeria. In a first attack, they kidnapped the wife of our deputy prime minister. The bodyguards only had time to protect her husband. In a second attack, the Boko Haram attackers carried out a massive raid. They rounded up everyone they came across: the local traditional chiefs and the ordinary villagers who were happily pounding their millet and sorghum and singing while they worked. The author of the article compares this raid to the kidnapping of the Chibok schoolgirls: they sweep through and destroy everything in their path. They don't even leave the scrawny sheep for the feast of Tabaski. Five dead and dozens missing. The journalist adds that the region has become so dangerous that several Western countries are advising their citizens not to visit Cameroon, or at least that area.

"And you say that's not serious?! Not *serious*! And with things like that going on you want us to go and look for Roger up in the north?"

"Ssssh! Do you want them to find out, is that it?"

"They've kidnapped the wife of the deputy prime minister. Just think! If they kidnap her, then we . . . No, but you're kidding, Simon! We'd better stay at home. I'm not going anywhere."

"Calm down, Johnny! Calm down and listen to me: one, we won't necessarily have to go all that way."

"What if Roger's already there . . . ?"

"Let me finish, will you?"

" . . ."

"One, we won't necessarily be going that far. Kolofata isn't around the corner, is it? And two, this isn't about me or you. It's about your brother. Everything we're doing here is for Roger. You need to get that into your head. We're doing it for Roger. And Roger's your brother before being mine. We're friends, like our parents. We're a family, right? Okay, so if you don't care about finding your brother and making your mother a little less unhappy, we can forget it. Yes, yes, tell me if that's what you want. Because if that's the case, it doesn't bother me. We can stay here in Douala, nice and safe. Too bad for Roger and especially for your mother."

"No, but . . ."

"There are no 'buts' . . . Is that what you want. Is it?"

7

We drive through Yassa, a neighborhood on the outskirts, at a snail's pace. The Security Voyage bus is a big vehicle, with around sixty seats in rows either side of a carpeted aisle. No one wears a seat belt. "The Whites really are strange!" exclaims an elephantine woman with a brightly colored headscarf. "These seat belts of theirs, what's the point of them, jooor?" She settles in. On her right are her two little boys whose heads are much bigger than their bodies.

I'm next to the window. Simon's on my left. I draw the curtain to dampen the harsh light; the March heat is unbearable. Inside the bus, we're all sweating like bakers' apprentices. Simon thinks he put a fan in one of our backpacks, but unfortunately, they're in the luggage compartment. He asks me to open the window: "It's stifling in here," he says. But the windows are sealed. The young hostess, whose body is as stale as an old carrot, explains with a superior expression that it's so we can get the maximum benefit from the air conditioning. And God alone knows whether this bus's air con system is working. In the meantime, Simon fans himself with a newspaper folded in half whose headline screams: "March 8: International Debauchery Day!"

Like all the other passengers, Simon wonders when we'll get out of this traffic jam. We've been stuck on this verge for nearly three-quarters of an hour. That's right, three-quarters of an hour and we haven't even gone one kilometer. There's hooting from all sides. The queues of cars are endless: the state of the road is the main cause. Our driver maneuvers as best he can, yanking the bus to the left, to the right, we nod our heads like those dogs on the rear shelf of a car and, *thank God*, we managed to avoid a huge pothole. A crater. The acrid smell of exhaust fumes irritates me. I cover my nostrils with a Kleenex for protection. The motorcycle taxis, carrying three, four, even five people, weave in and out of the narrow gaps. Very quickly, they end up filling the smallest space. The din is horrendous. People swear at one another: "Hey, you there, can't you wait like everyone else? Who gave you a driving license?" "Fuck your mother! Who do you think you are? Stupid idiot!" A third, a fourth, an umpteenth driver pitches in and the war of words intensifies. Everything has come to a standstill. The heat aggravates our driver's temper and makes him more impatient. He has productivity targets to meet. Who knows, perhaps he has to make a dozen return trips between Douala and Yaounde every day?

The road finally opens up. We turn onto the N3 Yaounde highway like mothers pouncing on new deliveries of clothing in Ndokoti market.

The driver hoots several times. "Dammit!" He has to ask the car in front to let him in. But it's no good. He accelerates and tries to force his way through. He brakes hard and we're all thrown against the seat in front. We're nose to tail with another crammed bus. Oh Yésu! Unbelievable. Voices clamor inside the vehicle criticizing the driver. "Even a dog can drive better than that!" complains a stocky guy with a bushy beard, adding: "With a head like that, he looks like an avocado stone!" The fat woman with the brightly colored headscarf shouts: "Hey driver! I've got two little-little kids here! If that's how you drive, excuse me, but let us off here. *Better* we continue on foot." People laugh. It's as if nothing has happened.

Death Highway, that's the N3's nickname. Hundreds of kilometers of asphalt and two lanes with nothing to separate them. At times, through the window, the forest is a solid green. Wrecked cars sit rusting by the roadside. Not far from the start of the town of Edea, a battered bus lies in the bushes. The scattered belongings and bloodstains show that the accident has just happened. A few hours ago, or at most one or two days. A little plyboard sign reads: "22 people died here."

Simon tells me that the N3 is one of the deadliest highways in the world. "*In the world*, I tell you!" He stresses the words to make sure I understand the seriousness of what he's saying. He complains that since Independence, no one has built a motorway on this stretch, even though it's the busiest in the country. Thousands of lorries, logging trucks, tankers and other haulage vehicles use it daily. It's the road from the port of Douala to the landlocked neighboring countries, especially Chad and the Central African Republic. He tells me that there are the occasional radar speed checks to encourage drivers to keep one foot on the brake. When I ask him whether these radars work, he shrugs: "And even if they did, do you think the money would go into the state coffers?"

We exchange a few more gibes about the driver's incompetence. Since leaving the traffic jams around Yassa behind us, he's alternated between crazy accelerations and slamming on the brakes, insults and outbursts of laughter, ill-humored gripes and sighs of relief.

For the first time since the start of our trip, I realize that Simon is scared. He buckles his seat belt and makes me do likewise. He takes out his blue Gideon New Testament and begins reading psalms, moving his lips like a goat chewing. He closes his eyes and crosses himself three or four times. I can't help laughing. I say: "If you're already afraid, driving along the Douala–Yaounde road, are you going to shit yourself at Kolofata?"

"Who says we're going to Kolofata?"

"I don't know. Maybe Kolofata will come to us. Who knows?"

"Shut up for Christ's sake! Concentrate on the journey."

Simon puts his New Testament in the string pocket on the back of the seat in front. I crease up. He looks at me and lets himself be infected by my laughter. Which annoys the obese woman with the brightly colored headscarf: "Honestly, respect has gone out of the window," she says and then tut-tuts endlessly.

Simon and I carry on laughing. Then Simon exclaims: "To think all this is because of Roger! Here we are on one of the most dangerous roads in the world: because of Roger. I'm sitting here praying and reading psalms like I never have before: because of Roger. Oh, Roger's quite something, I tell you!"

"What's more, you're not even certain he'll have you on his team when we find him."

"And supposing he selects you, then what, Johnny? I hope you'll score at least one goal, eh?"

We laugh ourselves silly. Our good humor spreads through the bus like wildfire. Soon, everyone's clutching their sides and stamping their feet. The fat lady's kids hoot even louder than us. But at least Simon and I know why we're laughing. It's an old story.

We were still just kids aged ten or twelve . . .

That is to say my big brother, like Pa, could spend hours and hours watching Champions League matches, but also all the other football competitions, including the lesser-known ones. The main thing for him was to see players chasing a ball. I've always found that ridiculous.

Roger founded a team, the Beedi Indomitable Eagles, of which he was captain. In Beedi, he was called Roger Milla. Now, in Cameroon, Roger Milla is a legend! He's the guy who led us into the quarter-final of the 1990 World Cup in Italy. Who doesn't remember him? His dribbles, his lightning kicks, his goals and especially his famous Makossa dance at the corner post, are part of our national history. Me, I remember it all as if it was yesterday, even though I wasn't born yet.

Everyone acknowledged that my brother Roger was brilliant at sports. And, in a country where football is a religion, he was proud of it. His talent had made him popular at a very young age. All the kids in Beedi hero-worshipped him. When he walked past, girls stopped chatting and gazed after him. It was quite a sight! Once he was out of view, they melted like margarine in the sun. They said: "Eeesh Ma! Did you see how fiiiiit he is? Ooooh!" or "Mmm! That guy's cuteness is totally gonna kill us!"

And what about me in all that? Oh, I didn't have my brother's aura! Not even a quarter of it! Football and me were like salt and an earthworm. All the same, Roger did his utmost to have me on his team. He wanted to share his glory with me. That's why he decided to have me play in the Beedi Football Champions League. It was was quite something, that championship! It involved the entire neighborhood and even the surrounding ones. Everyone came out to support the players as if they were family. The fans fought when the opponent's supporters called – or even thought of calling – their star a pussy. For fuck's sake!

Simon had been uneasy at the idea of me joining the Beedi Indomitable Eagles team. He knew I was hopeless: it was blindingly obvious.

Simon had said: "Hey, Roger, I'm not refusing to have Jean in our team, okay, but . . ."

"But what?" replied my brother. "But what?"

"But . . . it's . . . I mean . . . well, you know what I'm trying to say."

Roger was so well-loved in Beedi that you had to think very long and hard before arguing with him. Simon could have let the matter drop, but others – especially Mabingo, whose place I'd be taking – had encouraged him, albeit half-heartedly, to insist.

"I simply wanted to ask you . . . ," Simon began, "are you certain that Johnny knows how to kick a ball? Does he? We've never seen him actually play football. And we all know he doesn't like it. Are we going to force him to play for us? Let me remind you, Roger, that Jean is my little brother, too. So, it's not a question of jealousy or whatever. Honestly, in your shoes, I wouldn't have him on my team. Jean's good at a thousand other things, yes, a thousand other things, but not football. *I swear!* With him, we're bound to lose." The more Simon talked, the more Roger's face crumpled. It was as if Simon had called him a village-boy, a bastard or a sonofabitch! Roger's expression veered to outrage. Mabingo hung his head. We all hung our heads and listened hard, the better to hear our captain. The verdict came: harsh, to set an example. Simon was put on the substitutes' bench there and then. No quibbling. No. With Roger, no question of negotiating this sort of thing. No, no and no. How dare Simon attack his little brother head on, claiming he couldn't play football? No, really! There are times when things mustn't be said, for goodness' sake! Simon would be sitting on the subs' bench until pigs could fly. *And that was that!* Roger had sworn to leave him on the touchline for the duration of the Beedi Champion's League. But this was to ignore my very real ineptitude.

In the Beedi Football Champion's League, I'd inherited Mabingo's position, backup striker, just behind my brother, who was the lead striker: the goal scorer. Catapulting me in like that had caused grumbling among the rest of the team, particularly because I'd never taken part in any of their training sessions. I didn't understand their jargon. Maybe one or two words, but that was it. For example, they'd yell *touma* meaning "pass me the ball" or "send me the ball," or *mboundja!*: "Shoot, go on, shoot! Goal!"

From the first whistle, when they'd begun speaking their weird language, I was lost. They may as well have been speaking Chinese. Fifteen minutes later, a golden opportunity: we were playing against the Desert Marabouts and I was facing their goal, and I wasn't even offside. Aaah! Bébéto, the guy who'd replaced Simon as right midfielder, had the ball. From where he was, he could have scored easily – the defense wasn't in position. *Zero macabo!* Like a sieve, the Desert Marabouts team! But, instead of letting Bébéto go on to score and do a victory dance on the touchline, Roger had yelled "*Touma na* Jean! *Touma na* Jean!" and that's how I found myself, *I swear*, with the ball between my feet. Disaster! Oh how my brother would have liked to see me score, even if the ball had bounced off the goalpost. Then he could have crushed it into those guys' heads, but especially into the protester Simon's, that I, Jean Moussima Bobé, aka Johnny – like all the Moussima Bobés, both men and women – had football in my DNA! In our family, football has always run in our veins.

But faced with the Desert Marabouts' hulking goalie, my legs turned so weak that I scuffed the ground next to the ball: a huge clod of earth flew up, along with the nail from the big toe of my right foot. Which triggered a great burst of laughter from the opponents' goalie. Bitter humiliation!

But perhaps the worst thing was losing our match that day 1–0. Our very first match of the championship. And who did we lose to? Oh God, when I think about it . . . That's the most painful thing. Who did we lose to? Those pathetic little Desert Marabouts. The ultimate humiliation!

8

A few dozen meters before the Edea toll gate, the Security Voyage bus pulled up and parked on the scrubland beside the road. A horde of street pedlars descended on us at once, chasing after a handful of coins. From the youngest – barely ten years old – to the oldest, all were barking at us: "Coconut, coconut, two for one, two for one!" "Plantain chips, plantain chips!" "Condoms-bonbons-cigarettes! Condoms-bonbons-cigarettes!" Like a magician juggling spinning plates, a skinny girl holds out two bowls of bitter kola in her tiny hands. She's lost in her dress as floaty as a phantom sheet. She wants to be the first to spot potential customers. But she's still on the other side of the toll gate. She comes through, offering her wares to each more or less stationary car. "Bitter kola? Bitter kola, madame, a little bitter kola against stomachache?" I wonder how many times she goes back and forth in one day to sell her entire stock of bitter kola. She somehow manages not only to pick her way through the mass of vendors but also to weave between the vehicles that slow down at the speed bumps and police barriers. Suddenly, a squeal of brakes. My stomach lurches. The girl was almost run over by a motorcycle taxi; the hem of her tunic is ripped, but that doesn't worry her. More important are her kolas. "Bitter kola? Hey, Pa! A little bitter kola to rouse you?" And now she's continuing her mission, crazy and heedless. Smiling.

Because the windows of our bus won't open, we have to get out to buy food. Several of us take advantage to stretch our legs or pee. All around us are countless little stalls under tents with roofs of plaited palm leaves. People are eating, smoking, drinking, laughing and arguing inside. It's teeming with life! Dozens of families live on their wits. How would they survive without this toll gate? It's the epicenter of their existence. The mothers peel green oranges artistically. With a sharp knife they cut thin strips from the skin then send their children off to sell them to the travellers. It's three oranges for a hundred francs. No bargaining: take it or leave it. Those little hands also offer cassava bread with palm oil – *mintoumba* – with grilled or caramelized groundnuts, palm wine, plantain chips, ginger juice or hibiscus tea and more.

Simon asks me what I fancy. Grilled caterpillars would do me a lot of good. When he gets off the bus, I notice however that he goes off wiggling his bum. So much for the caterpillars – he's most likely looking for a bush where he can relieve himself.

Some passengers leave the bus for good. They've reached their destination. Others buy a ticket before boarding. They're going to Boumnyebel, Mbankomo or Yaounde. The driver and his motorboy stow the bags on the roof of the bus and in the baggage compartment. There's never enough room for all the luggage. A toothless old woman chides the motorboy: "Do want to kill my son's hens or what, hmmm? If they don't arrive in Yaounde alive and happy, you'll wish you'd never been born! I'm the one who's telling you." Her threat ringing in his ears, the driver's assistant and gofer makes sure he places the conical raffia basket holding the poor hens carefully on the roof.

Lots more chatter, screeching, a few protracted arguments and some jostling. The driver himself disappears for a while to go and pay the toll. The toll-collectors wear satchels stuffed with bank notes. The state won't see even a third of their daily takings.

That's it. Everyone's settled at last. The engine rumbles into action: we're ready to set off again. But Simon still hasn't come back. Oh God! I signal to the hostess that there's a passenger missing. She looks me up and down and shrugs: "If he'd bought food from us on board, we wouldn't have had this problem." The bus doors close. It's too late. I call out to the hostess, the motorboy and the driver: "Hey! Wait . . . wait! Hey! Wait! My brother isn't back!" The engine stops. A loud ripple of annoyance. Someone yells that they don't give a fuck! "No time to waste, driver! Let's go!" The stocky man with the bushy beard shouts: "I hope he'll at least wash his hands before getting back on the bus." Everyone laughs. The driver exchanges a look with the motorboy and the hostess. Irritated, he starts up again. The bus slowly moves off. It lurches onto the road. I get up. I yell. I stamp my feet. I protest. "Hey, driver! Wait! Wait, oh! . . . Wait!" The fat lady with the headscarf yells, too. She says we have to wait for Simon. Other women plead on my behalf. "We can't leave without his brother! What is it with you? You're behaving as if you don't have children, too." The bus is split into two camps: the men, who want us to leave, versus the women who refuse to abandon Simon. They don't have the chance to confront each other, insults for insults, profanities for profanities, because already someone's banging on the bus door: it's Simon.

Phew!

Simon is sweating. I thought he'd gone off for a pee, but here he is, breathless, holding a packet of grilled caterpillars. He's also bought two cans of Heineken and a bottle of mineral water. "Is it for beer that you wasted our time?" complains the driver, setting off again with a jolt. "What beers?!? He wanted to fuck a village girl, that's all!" chimes in one passenger. Another burst of laughter. The men reprimand the latecomer. The woman with the headscarf tells Simon to give her a little something: "Ask your brother. If it hadn't been for me, they'd have left you here in the Bassas' forest. You owe me two thousand francs, including tax. And watch out, I'm not joking!" Her kids with the oversized heads are laughing, revealing their gappy milk teeth.

"So, what happened Simon, eh?"

He tells me he bought grilled caterpillars quite close to the bus, but that he had to go all the way to the village bar to get Heineken. It's a lot cheaper there than by the bus, where it's a rip-off. And then he took his chance to pursue our investigation. He asked the bar owner whether he'd heard of a certain Roger Moussima Bobé. The guy scratched his temple. "Roger Moussima Bobé?" No, it didn't ring a bell. But Simon showed him a photo of Roger on his smartphone. "Look! This is him. This is my brother. Have a good look." The owner called his waitress over. She glanced at the photo and simpered. Simon knows the local codes and gave her a five-hundred CFA note, which she slipped into her bra. Roger Moussima Bobé, now she recognized the name. Around three or four months ago, she'd seen him in the area. Liar! Roger had run away only a month ago.

Serves Simon right. He should have been more cautious. People have no qualms about making money out of another person's misfortune. His mother, Sita Bwanga, was forever telling him. One man's loss is another man's gain. So here we are, only at the start of our journey, and Simon has wasted money on fake info. Dammit, he could have bought me two extra packets of grilled caterpillars with those five hundred francs! And to think we nearly left him behind in that forest region for that nonsense . . . Jesus!

But the thing is, Simon didn't let her get away with it. "You know me, don't you Johnny? You know me," he says with an ounce of pride. He demanded his money back from the waitress. At first politely. Such a gentleman! Then he raised his voice like a Bantu warrior. So then the owner wanted to throw him out. "Go on, off with you. Out of here!" Simon refused. He pinned the waitress against a door and tried to fish the money out of her bra. At that, the bar owner became enraged as if he'd seen the devil in person. He yelled "*Bad luck!* What? I'm going to count to three . . ." He inserted his thumb and forefinger between his lips and whistled. A group of heavies arrived, shaved heads, brandishing clubs. Poor Simon! He had to get out of there as fast as he could if he wanted to hold on to all his teeth.

9

Despite the driver's brutal steering, we finally reach Yaounde. As she gets off, the lady with the headscarf blesses her ancestors and the heavens. The toothless old woman checks her son's hens are still alive and, above all, happy! She smiles at the motorboy, revealing her black gums. As each person retrieves their luggage, the fat woman with the headscarf turns to Simon and says: "My son, you owe me two thousand CFA. Don't forget that if it wasn't for me, they'd have left you behind at Edea. Seeing as it's you, I'll let you off this time. But only this time, all right? But one-day one-day, you'll have to pay me." We part company, laughing. The lady tells us to take care. "It's dangerous out there, boys. Very dangerous!" she adds, before disappearing with her sons, who look like the Rugrats.

The Security Voyage agency is opposite the Karibou university complex, a big blue-white building utterly devoid of charm. All around, the smell of youth. It's buzzing with energy and vitality. A whole host of enthusiastic and talented souls study here, but with the sole ambition of leaving this campus as quickly as possible. Leave! Get away at all costs. Go to *Mbeng*. Go to the Whites' country even if it means risking *boza*, even with their degree under their belt. Especially with a degree. You have to leave if you want a future. In this country, they likely say to themselves, they'll become nothing. Nothing at all.

Sita Mpondo, one of Ma's cousins, is waiting for us at the main entrance of this private university, lolling against her red Toyota Starlet. We don't spot her until she whirls her arms at us: "Hey boys! Boys? Jean! Simon! Yoo hoo!" We walk faster.

Her face doesn't have a single wrinkle. She looks like a pear, still slim on top but heavily curved below. Huge sunglasses crush her little nose. She has a magnificent Afro. In her beige checked blouse and dark-brown flared trousers, she looks as if she's just stepped out of a 1970s women's magazine. She opens her arms wide as if to engulf us. And then come lengthy embraces and routine greetings. She's constantly amazed. "How you've grown, little Johnny, haven't you?!" Then to Simon: "His mother Bwanga's wonder boy. Eh? You've shot up as fast as a papaya tree!"

"How was the journey?" she asks. We don't mention the episode at the Edea toll gate or our anxiety over the driver's recklessness. After all the hugging, she puts our backpacks in the boot. My God! The heat is indescribable. Whereas the Security Voyage bus that brought us from Douala to Yaounde had a semblance of air conditioning, Sita Mpondo's tiny Toyota Starlet is a furnace. My T-shirt is soaked the minute I get into the car. Our auntie exclaims:

"Hey boys, you must be hungry!" You can say that again. But Simon and I are reluctant to admit it. Simon even goes so far as to say "we're fine, we're fine," adding that we had some grilled caterpillars and they were still crawling around in our stomachs. But Sita Mpondo is insistent: "Only some measly caterpillars? That's not enough for big boys like you." Hallelujah! Now I take the initiative and tell her we are hungry. Oh yes, auntie! "My tummy's even singing the cha-cha-cha."

We get out of the car right away. Sita Mpondo offers to take us to the most popular local tourne-dos. That's what the roadside restaurants are called because customers eat with their backs to the road. These days, people want to avoid being recognized. If someone sees you eating, they barge in. Don't they say that if there's enough for one, there must be enough for ten?

Sita Mpondo swears that this tourne-dos is a must. The woman who owns the place is such a good cook that sometimes she herself, Sita Mpondo, buys her husband's dinner there. And when she does, he's doubly complimentary. She waggles her finger and says: "I don't want to hear that my secret is out, okay? Are we agreed?"

My aunt taking us to a tourne-dos reminds me of my early days at the university.

It was a Monday, a few months ago. The previous day, Simon had arranged to meet me on the campus. He'd asked me to wait for him in front of the basketball court. It was two o'clock and I stood watching the strapping guys with bulging muscles playing. Funny sport. I don't get it at all. Actually, football's the only game whose rules I at least know.

Simon hadn't shown up and I had no credit left on my phone to call him, so I had to stay put and wait. Around me, the campus: the patches of grass eaten away and neglected, a few decrepit buildings covered in thick layers of dust and cobwebs. On my left, the big gymnasium that serves as a lecture theater for classes – especially for the freshers. There are so many of them that there isn't enough room for everyone on the bench-desks inside. To get a seat, you have to arrive very early in the morning, at around five. Otherwise you have to make do with a breezeblock outside.

From where I stood, I could hear the voice of the lecturer in the big gymnasium. That room, in normal times, should have been home to the young basketball players. The surrounding noise, both outside and inside the gymnasium, drowned out the lecturer's voice even though he was using a loudspeaker.

Simon arrived more than half an hour later.

"So sorry, little Johnny! We had practicals for the microeconomics class. The assistant took up a bit more time than usual."

"No problem. Was it good?"

"It was okay. I just have to pass this one and my degree's in the bag. What about you? You look a bit tired..."

"The first year's tough, you know."

"I can help you if you like. Don't be afraid to ask, right?"

Simon waved in the direction he wanted us to take to leave the campus. I'd told him about my difficulties with math. Things were getting better and better, but it wasn't really my cup of *bissap*. I'd so much rather be studying something like . . . I don't know, the arts, communication or psychology . . . "I dunno, something like that, you know what I mean." Then he asked me why I'd chosen economics. "It's my mother," I said, hanging my head as if in shame.

"Ah, I see, I see: 'He who pays the piper calls the tune,' right?"

"You've got it."

As we left the campus, I looked around at the posters on the walls extolling the benefits of studying in Europe.

In the first year, a natural selection operated. Many students ended up dropping out. Either they found the enrollment fees too high – 75,000 CFA a semester: the price of a brand-new Samsung Galaxy S5! – or were disheartened by the appalling study conditions. A lot of girls opted for marriage, children, lots of children, family. Others chose to run away in search of Eldorado. That's why all over the campus you saw posters advertising the advantages of studying in Europe – in other words Ukraine, Turkey, Azerbaijan or Uzbekistan! The posters showed attractive White students, fair hair for the girl, dark for the young man. Clutching binders, they had the radiant smiles of assured success. The backdrop was always an urban landscape: a luminous glass skyscraper beside a lake or a turquoise pond; lush greenery. And the slogans: "Azerbaijan! The key to success." Or: "Odessa, the university for you." Many students were ripped off in these idiotic scams. They paid a fortune to middlemen who vanished without trace. The more business-like agents – God alone knows how many there are – abandoned the students to fend for themselves in Uzbekistan. Several had come back bruised, ashamed, disillusioned, empty-handed.

Then Simon invited me to eat in a tourne-dos, Chez Mamie Yossa: a corrugated-iron roof nailed onto four poles planted in the ground. Beneath this tent, several dozen students. The place was packed out. The din was like a market. Mamie Yossa's rivals said that her tourne-dos attracted so many *asso* – punters – because she put slivers of witchcraft in her cooking pots. They even said that Mamie Yossa certainly poured in some of her red wine that women piss out every month. Aaah, the gossip! But you simply had to look at Mamie Yossa to see that her cellar's run dry, and had done a long time ago! Isn't that why they call her *mamie*? Despite all the rumors, Mamie Yossa's place is always full. Finally, all this *kongossa*, this bad-mouthing, this tittle-tattle, only brought her more customers. The more people said that . . . The more people said they'd heard that . . . the busier Mamie Yossa's tourne-dos was.

In one of the four corners of the tent, fat Mamie Yossa stirred her pots. She was so misshapen that, in comparison, a hippopotamus could take up modeling. While she held the ladle, a gazelle-waitress wrote down the orders, took the money and then served the food. The heat from the wood fire added to that of the sun, beating down on the corrugated iron over our heads. Not even a light breeze to bring some relief.

While we were eating, shouting broke out, making me jump. People were yelling at a young man from the north: a Maghida. You can recognize the Maghida by their thin, lithe shape and their very dark skin. That's what our schoolbooks say. The Maghida roll their *r*'s in in a way that identifies them immediately. At the Conquête du Savoir private college, my history teacher had taught us that these people are thin because they live in the desert and semi-desert regions of the north. Instead of eating their livestock (because they are mainly cattle farmers), they let them graze. They're always looking for a little patch of green grass for their animals, or a watering hole. True or false? I have no idea. What I retained was that people from the north aren't like us, people of the south, who've become obese from our diet of cassava and palm oil.

The Maghida at Mamie Yossa's tourne-dos accused us of taking advantage of the terrorist threat affecting the far north region. He said that people were dying every day in Boko Haram attacks, while the southerners remained indifferent. And the other students replied: "*Aka!* To hell with you and your cows! Let us eat in peace. Back off!" But the young Maghida wouldn't let it go: "Again yesterday, a young man died of his wounds in my village, in Banki. But no one's talking about that. *Wallaï*, it's not right!"

"You, where do you get your news from, bro?" a student with a spotty forehead had asked.

"I *wanda* about him," added another with rabbit ears. "He surprises me."

"Is there any more groundnut soup?!"

"*I beg!* Go and argue away from my tourne-dos!"

"Leave that Maghida alone unless you want him to turn you into a cow tail!"

The entire restaurant erupted in a great roar of laughter. Some were stamping their feet and clutching their sides. A thin film of dust had settled on us.

"He'd better not come in here banging on about terrorist threats. We're not in Nigeria here, are we?"

"Nooo!"

"My brother, this is the Cameroon of Papa Biya. We're never gonna get this terrorism you're on about."

"Boko Haram are already here and we're turning a blind eye."

"Hey, m'amoiselle, what's happening? Where's my rice and groundnut soup!"

"The Maghida's hungry! Starvation drove him from his village."

"Give him a plate of rice. It's on me!" More helpless laughter.

"Idiots!" the Maghida fumed.

"Are you insulting me?"

"What are you going to do to me? Huh? You can't do anything to me!"

"He's *impeubable*!" taunted another customer. "You can't do anything to him."

"*Aka!* I don't care. Let the northerners keep their suffering to themselves. What's your problem? It's no big deal. As for us in the south, our parents died from the White man's colonization while you in the north were asleep – sleeping peacefully with your cows and your sheep. So don't you come here and give us grief!"

Simon laughed. He said: "*Kaï walaï!* Whatever you do, don't annoy a Maghida, or you're done for." I laughed, listening to him mimic the accent. The Maghida had left Mamie Yossa's tourne-dos swearing never to set foot there again. He'd insulted everyone on his way out and promised that Allah would punish us harshly.

That was the first time, six months ago, that I'd heard talk of the terrorist threat in Cameroon. In Mamie Yossa's tourne-dos.

10

Now, Sita Mpondo is insisting we should stop our mothers worrying. We phone them. Simon, first, talks to both of them on speakerphone. Yes, we had a good journey. No, we haven't seen Roger. Not yet. But it won't be long. On the other end of the line, tension must be sky-high. Simon doesn't dare say that we haven't picked up a single clue as to Roger's whereabouts. A brief silence. "Who have you met? Where? What have people told you? Is it true that Roger's making his way to France?" Sita Mpondo wants him to lie. Simon gives an evasive answer. But yes, that's right . . . well, for now . . . So people are saying . . . but he can't say much more. He puts on a grave air that makes me smile. He's like Columbo preoccupied by a very, very complicated case.

When I take the phone to talk to Ma, she bursts into tears. I just say: "Big kisses, Ma. Everything's fine here. We'll find him." "Be brave, my Choupi! Courage, my little Choupinours." I try to say something more.

She's already hung up.

Sita Mpondo bows her head. Simon gazes at one of the town's seven distant hills. My eyes mist over. "Noooo, my love!" says Sita Mpondo, putting her arms around me.

"You mustn't cry. You're a big boy, aren't you? We'll do our utmost to find Roger. And the Good Lord and your father's spirit up there will help us. You'll see. Everything will be fine. Come on! Stop crying now. Okay?"

We don't have time to digest our okra with rice couscous. We don't even have time to digest the emotion of the conversation with our mothers and already Sita Mpondo wants to take us to the police station. One of her friends is having it off with the local police chief. "He's a nice man," she says emphatically, then adds: "I've never met him, but I know that he's a good guy. He'll help us." Simon doesn't seem thrilled at the idea. Hadn't Sita Bwanga asked us to keep the police well out of this business? If he ignored his mother's advice, what happened to him at the Edea toll gate might be repeated.

We must follow our mothers' advice to avoid traps. But Sita Mpondo's our mother, too, isn't she?

Sita Mpondo quickly understands our lack of enthusiasm. Our exhaustion. She sighs: "Don't worry, boys. Come on! There are police and police in this country. Okay? I've already spoken to my sisters Bwanga and Moussima about it. I know this police very, very well. Even if I've never seen him, the superintendent, the chief of the chiefs of the central police station, Monsieur Éyoum, is the *sponsor* of a very close friend of mine. He promised to help me. I give you my word! He promised me. I called him again this morning. He told me he wasn't in his office but that he would leave instructions with the chief inspector, a woman. So relax, boys! Trust me. Okay?"

"Auntie," Simon begins, without looking at her. "If we go to this police station, it's to do what, concretely?"

"Ah that I don't know! I'm not a superintendent or an inspector, or any such thing. I don't even know what happens when a person runs away. They might put out a missing person's appeal, no? That's the least they can do. Announcements on the TV, the radio, in the newspapers . . . in any case, they'll do something. And then you, you're young, aren't you? Why haven't you posted a message on Facebook?"

It hadn't even crossed my mind. What an idiot! I'd only noticed that there'd been no postings on Roger's account since the day he left.

Simon promised to explore that avenue once we got back to Sita Mpondo's. It would be very quick and, why not, we'd be able to gather information without necessarily having to pay anything.

Meanwhile, we trust our auntie. She drives us to Yaounde's central police station.

It's two single-story buildings opposite each other. The paintwork, which should be white and baby blue, has turned an ocher, red-dust color. A tangle of electric wires hangs exposed. Inspector Fouda's office is very untidy. No maintenance in the dark corridors. When was a broom or a rag last used on this floor? Everywhere, yellowing, damp, curling papers. Spiders had spun elaborate webs – the only works of art in the room. A barely finished plate of rice sits moldering under the eyes of the female inspector. She's even made it her temporary bin. Cigarette butts jostle for space with chewing-gum wrappers. She makes no attempt to hide this mess when we sit down facing her, even though the smell is unbearable. It's as if she's lost her sense of smell. Eeesh!

The ceiling fan hisses above our heads. A lot of straining for nothing: the room is boiling hot.

"I am Madame Mpondo," begins Auntie, disgusted at the squalor.

"Ah, Madame Mpondo," replies the inspector in a sing-song voice, crossing her arms over her sunken chest. She must have noticed our embarrassment, but she continues to smile as if nothing's wrong.

"Yes. Superintendent Éyoum asked me to come in and see you today."

"Yes, yes. He told me about this problem of a runaway. Is that why you're here?"

"That's right. My son Roger, Roger Moussima Bobé. He ran away more than a month ago, and we've had no news since."

"A month you say, is that so?"

"Yes, a month," replies Simon, trying to edge his way into the conversation.

Inspector Fouda has put her plate-bin back under the desk. But the foul smell lingers. She takes a used toothpick out of a drawer and begins scrupulously cleaning her teeth. She does it so pointedly that her gesture looks like a deliberate attempt at provocation. I glower at her in disgust: her skin is such a dirty black, so filthy that I wonder when she last had a shower.

"One short month is too soon to start worrying."

"But inspector . . . already a whole month!" protests Sita Mpondo, wagging her forefinger. "You must have children, too. Haven't you? Could you go such a long time without news?"

"Madame um . . . Madame Mpondo? Is that right?"

"Yes, Mpondo."

"Well, Madame Mpondo, I'll stop you right there. You haven't come here to talk about my children and how I've raised them. Because, you see, if you'd raised your son properly, he would never have run away without sending word. So I'm not going to take lessons from anyone, especially not you."

The already strained atmosphere turns icy. What a counterattack! An exchange of stunned glances between Simon, Auntie and me. Total silence. Only the ceiling fan hisses and stirs up a reddish dust. Sita Mpondo takes a deep breath before venturing: "It's possible he's heading for Europe. Are you familiar with those networks?"

"He wants boza?" sniggers the woman. "How old?"

"Twenty."

"Twenty and already he wants boza . . . There! That's what I was saying! When we ask parents to keep their children under control . . . It's a matter of upbringing, Madame Mpondo. Do you understand? That's what I was telling you earlier."

I watch Simon. If she hadn't been a police inspector, he'd have shut her up ages ago, that filthologist bitch. What am I saying? He's not able to do anything. He couldn't even stand up for himself against a waitress at the Edea toll gate. Faced with this filthologist inspector, he won't be any smarter.

Sita Mpondo takes it on the chin. Poor thing! And when we'd arrived, she'd been so eager. "Is it not possible to put out a missing person appeal or something?" Her stifled anger makes her voice hoarse. "Put ads in the newspapers, mention it on the TV and radio news . . . do you see what I mean?"

The inspector explodes with laughter. Which leaves us speechless. Now, even I can no longer stand her, that filthy bitch. *She's seriously getting on my nerves!* I want only one thing: for us to get the hell out.

"Madame Mpondo! Oh, Madame Mpondo. Forgive me for laughing like that. I'm not laughing at you. No. But what you're saying is so funny. It's even the funniest thing I've ever heard." She gets her breath back and starts cleaning her teeth with the toothpick again, then adds: "How could you have thought for a single second that our station – Yaounde's central police station! – would be willing to mobilize so many resources to look for a little brat hankering after Europe? Be reasonable, madame! Is he the son of our Papa-President? And even if he were . . . You have no idea how much the smallest search operation costs. Would you be prepared to spend millions to find a little moron?"

"But . . . ," Sita Mpondo protests.

"But what? What? Do you want us to alert Interpol for a . . . for a . . . a badly brought-up boy?"

"How dare you call my son badly brought-up! How dare you!"

"Madame . . ."

"Now look, just because you're wearing a uniform, that doesn't give you the right to do or say anything you want."

"Like mother, like son! And now Madame Mpondo is teaching me my job! And just because you know Superintendent Éyoum, do you think that gives you the right to disrespect a police officer?"

"I have not disrespected you, Inspector. What I want is for you to help me find my son . . ."

"We are both women and mothers. And we know what that's like. Your little game stops where mine begins. Okay? So, take it up with Superintendent Éyoum and we'll see if you're a *real* woman."

I put my hand on Auntie's thigh to pacify her. I can't take any more of this filthologist bitch, please Auntie! Simon's mind is on other things, and he looks downcast. Sita Mpondo threatens to take the matter up to the chief commissioner. "Go ahead, madame! Go ahead! And what else? Go and see our Papa-President in person and his wife, Ma Chantou! Even go and talk to the pope if you like! What nonsense! What difference do you think that will make? Crazy! Foolish woman! We have a lot to deal with at this station. Believe it or not, there are priorities! We look after our citizens' safety. We aren't paid to go after badly brought-up little troublemakers dreaming of Europe."

We stood up, deeply disappointed and upset. It really should be their job to carry out investigations of this sort here. Aaah! If only Sita Bwanga were here to remind us that you can't trust the police in this country. In the dusty yard of the police station, there were motorcycle taxis and two or three impounded vehicles. "You there, madame! Madame Mpondo!" It was the inspector woman. As we turned toward her, all three of us hoped that she finally had something concrete to say to us or even that she'd ask us for an "envelope" for her to consider our request: we could have talked about it. But no, that filthy bitch shouted at us: "That son of yours, let him die in his boza! Our country doesn't want any more of his kind! Got it? To hell with you!"

Some uniformed men sitting on the veranda, bottle of beer in hand and cigarette in mouth, started sniggering. They shouted: "Inspector Fouda! Inspector Fouda! Who's got you all annoyed? Tell us and we'll lock them up right away!"

"Forget it boys! Forget it! A madwoman who comes in acting all Mr. Clean in my office! She has the cheek to come here and preach to me. Is she daydreaming or what? Did someone tell her I was a cleaner? I'm an inspector, for goodness' sake! When we ask them to keep an eye on their kids, they talk their talk-talk. Then they come whining to me. Outrageous! Let her go and see Éyoum if she's a *real* woman!"

Another outburst of laughter that follows us all the way to Sita Mpondo's Toyota Starlet. It was so humiliating!

11

Twenty years' slaving under his belt and at last my father was promoted to production manager at the SABC. At least, that's what he said. It took me a while to understand that Pa had given himself that title, because in actual fact he was *only* the assistant manager. A fair-haired little Frenchman from France, newly graduated from an engineering school in Grenoble, had snatched his position. Pa cursed: "They've sent us a little idiot. He doesn't even drink alcohol! Just think! The kid doesn't even drink! And he's the one who'll be explaining to me things that he doesn't understand – to me, who's been making beer since prehistoric times?"

And Ma would reply: "Oh Claude, my husband! When I talk to you, you always say that I exaggerate, that I go round and round in circles. And now look! Do you think that sitting there with your arms folded will get you promoted to manager? Do you? No way! You have to make an effort, do something. Otherwise they'll get a kid barely out of kindergarten to give you a kick up your backside."

"And what does madame expect me to do?"

"You have to *be nice* to your bosses!"

"*Be nice* to my bosses? Aren't they loaded enough?"

"People can never have enough money! And it's me, your wife, Ngonda Moussima Bobé, telling you."

Ma had rolled up the sleeves of her kaba ngondo as if she was about to set about a difficult chore. Then she went on in a quiet voice: "Look at your colleague Monkam, who started not even a year ago; he's already sales manager."

"So what?!"

"How do you think he did it?"

"Tell me what he did, since you know everything."

"Oh darling, anyone would think you were born yesterday! Give them crates of champagne! Bung them envelopes, all of them, from the most junior to the big boss. And if you can't, let me take care of it. Don't they say that behind every great man is an even greater woman? I am already that woman, hiding behind the boss I want you to become."

"Oh Ngonda, you're crazy! You need to see an exorcist."

"Hold a party for them, a reception, something . . . I don't know . . . but do something. In the meantime, I'll go and see the pastor and ask the Good Lord for a miracle."

"The Good Lord . . . The Good Lord . . . Give them champagne . . . Give them this, give them that . . . While we're about it, I can give you to the little White man, too. Because it always begins with bottles of champagne, then ends up with my wife in the boss's bed. Doesn't it? That's the way things work here."

"Oh Yésu! Now that's warped thinking! What's he talking about? I'm trying to show him what to do to get himself promoted and he comes out with this nonsense."

In actual fact, Ma didn't care whether Pa was manager or *only* assistant production manager at SABC. What she wanted was the salary that went with a managerial post. She needed a lot of money to move house. Ma wanted to get out of Beedi at all costs. Hadn't Sita Mpondo bought herself a brand-new, single-storey detached house? Hadn't our poor neighbor Sita Bwanga built her White House? If those two women, who were in no way her equals, had managed to buy themselves proper homes, then why should she, Ngonda Moussima Bobé, be condemned to live in a prefab in Beedi?

At the beginning of the 2000s, with government support, the Société Immobilière du Cameroun, the SIC, launched ambitious housing projects in Douala and Yaounde. The SIC built apartment blocks and detached and semi-detached houses. The authorities trumpeted that we were emerging: "Cameroon has great ambitions!" "Cameroon is achieving great things!" They swore, hand on heart, their expressions oozing sincerity, that never again would we lag behind when it came to development! No longer would people be huddled together like rats in the slum districts, the sôlô-quarters.

With Pa's half-promotion, Ma could at last hope to leave. Right away, if possible. But Pa thought the move too expensive: he was *only* assistant manager, remember! "Then you should have become manager," retorted Ma, her fists planted on her thighs. That's how they argue, for entire evenings. With no half-time. Both refusing to drop their guard.

Pa might well fly, fly and fly, but eventually, like a sparrow, he always felt the need to come to rest on the branches of the tree that was his Ngonda Moussima Bobé. So he bought her a detached SIC house in Bonamoussadi.

Our new house was exactly the same as Sita Mpondo's: the same sliding metal gate, the same living room and adjoining dining room, two bedrooms, a kitchen at the back and so on.

"It's just like Sita Moussima's house," exclaims Simon, inspecting every inch of it. Sita Mpondo and I burst out laughing. I give Simon a blow-by-blow account of the purchase of our house in Bonamoussadi. More laughter, then Simon gets up and races to the toilet. "What's wrong?" asks Sita Mpondo. "Have you got a stomachache? I hope it's not the food from the tourne-dos."

"No!" yells Simon from the toilet. "It's that bitch of an inspector!"

Despite everything, our mood lightens, even though Sita Mpondo is still shocked that the inspector thinks she sleeps with the chief of police. "It's outrageous that you have to give your ass to a high-up someone to be a *real* woman."

Simon comes out of the toilet and begs auntie to forget the filthologist bitch. "We told you to keep the police well out of this business. Now at least it's clear: we'll have to manage on our own."

Sita Mpondo connects her Huawei Wi-Fi modem.

Simon immediately posts a photo of Roger on Facebook, the same one we've been using since the start of our inquiries. And he adds the following missing person appeal: "Dear friends, we've had no news of our brother and friend, Roger Moussima Bobé, for more than one month. Please contact us via Messenger if you have any information. Thank you for sharing this appeal. We need your help. Thank you again."

Sita Mpondo has retreated to her room. She's on the telephone, hooting with laughter. She's telling her friend about the scene at the Yaounde central police station. I get the impression she's chatting to the friend who's rumored to be sleeping with Superintendent Éyoum.

Like Simon, I'm glued to my phone. We're waiting for the replies to our post. Comments quickly arrive, including several RIPs, which annoy us. Simon has to respond that as far as we know Roger isn't dead. A missing person appeal isn't a death notice, you idiots! A few minutes later, the number of comments falls. Fewer *likes*, too. Anyway, how can people *like* such a sad post? On the other hand, the number of shares multiplies at incredible speed. In less than an hour, our status has been shared more than seven hundred times!

While waiting for information that seems reliable, Simon shows me videos on YouTube where Cameroonian girls from Paris hurl insults at each other. *Oh là là!* They call each other sluts, whores, lesbiwhores, smelly-ass'd bitches, *pimentières* who sell their asses for ten euros in basements or mobile homes. They crisscross the whole of France in search of *cli-cli* – either good old White men who are into Black tigresses, or prepubescent boys seeking their first steamy experience. We find these videos unbelievably ridiculous, but still spend ages watching them and laughing. We end up almost forgetting why Sita Mpondo has given us twenty thousand CFAs' worth of internet credit.

But while we're corrupting our ears listening to these pithy exchanges of insults, Simon receives a message from a profile in the name of the White Queen. This White Queen says she's seen Roger. When? About a week ago, or a bit more. What was he doing? Where was he? Is he still in Yaounde? No reply. She can't tell us anything on Facebook, The boss watches everything. If we believe her, we must go to Mini Ferme Melen, in the center of Yaounde, to find out more. Go to the Passe-Passe bar and ask to speak to Benghazi Omar: he has information about Roger. Does she have a phone number? Her fake profile won't give one. Simon presses her. Again, she refuses. The White Queen wishes to sever all contact with us. The only little bit of help: we can tell Benghazi Omar that she sent us.

Simon and I look at each other, openmouthed in disbelief.

Simon asks the White Queen where exactly the Mini Ferme Melen district is. And the Passe-Passe bar? He tells her that he comes from Douala and doesn't know Yaounde. *We're likely to get fleeced if we say too much about ourselves, buddy. Do you really think those thugs don't know what's going down on their turf? We've already been ripped off at least twenty times, I'm certain of it.* All the no-go districts are well organized, by gangs. In Beedi, in Ngodi-Akwa . . . and without any doubt also in their Mini Ferme Melen. Another message to the White Queen and we find out, to our dismay, that she's blocked us. No further contact.

All the same, we're quite pleased with this hook-up. Her profile photo tells us little about her identity. All you can see, in place of the head, is a wad of CFA banknotes and wraps of powder. Some joker's probably trying to screw us, hiding behind the anonymity of Facebook.

And what about this Benghazi Omar? Doesn't he sound like a dangerous guy?

Like kids, we call our mother Sita Mpondo. So she can tell us what she thinks of it all.

12

From the Olembe housing project, somewhere in the north of the city, we take a taxi for Mini Ferme Melen. It is nearly midnight. A power outage has just plunged the entire city in darkness. A darkness that nothing lightens, not the fireflies nor the headlights, nor the hurricane lamps of the street vendors.

In a traffic jam at Messassi market, the driver turns to Simon and me and sniggers: "Hey, you say you're going to Mini Ferme. Is that right, kids?" Simon mutters a vague yes. And from the driver's expression, we gather that Mini Ferme must be a hotspot. So then Simon asks the driver point blank if he knows the Passe-Passe bar. "Kids, I can't know every brothel in town!" he says with a sweep of his arm. "It's a hot-hot spot, you'd have to spend your nights munching butt to know all the names by heart! Given my age, I only go to Mini Ferme once in a blue moon. I'm fifty years old, guys! Fifty!" Simon, slightly embarrassed, opens the window. The driver's smoking. There's beeping on all sides.

On the main roads, the bars blare out the latest bikutsi hit:

"J'ai envie de . . . envie de . . . j'ai envie de faire!"
"I want . . . I want . . . I want to do it!"

A grilled-mackerel vendor pours her smelly fish water onto the road. It just misses us. The driver yells and the woman bawls at him: "Fuck your mother!"

Throwing his cigarette end into the gutter, the taximan thinks it helpful to tell us: "Hey boys, it makes no difference whether you go to your Passe-Passe or not. In Mini Ferme, there are girls everywhere. And I mean *everywhere*! Don't worry, you'll find a good lay, and not expensive!"

We're past the traffic jam between Messassi and Emana. After a few minutes, we turn down a narrow street that leads to the Nkol Eton road, then we drive toward Bastos. Bastos, easily recognizable: one of the city's most affluent neighborhoods. Perhaps *the* most affluent, with several embassies and consulates. All is quiet here. The rare girls in high heels on the roadside are targeting a wealthy clientele. Oh! The pimentières, the tarts! I can't help thinking about the exorbitant cost of having a patch of pavement here. Who rents it to them? What percentage of each trick do they have to pay? And what about the state coffers in all this? Dammit! Just when I want to ask Simon all these questions, the taximan turns up the volume of a Nigerian song that's taking the country by storm: *Dorobucci*. We don't understand a word of it, but the music is so frenzied it makes you want to shake your bum to the rhythm. Simon and I dance with our heads, repeating the chorus: *Oya doro . . . Dorobucci o! O Dorobucci o!* Lots of people are saying on social media that this song has a subliminal, even satanic, message. Ma's pastor has banned his followers from listening to such preaching direct from hell. Meanwhile, sorry Pastor

Njoh Solo, the driver, Simon and I carry on *dorobucci-ing* at the tops of our voices.

Nearly thirty minutes later, the driver parks in a busy street. "This is the road to the infamous Melen, kids!" he says with a smile. Then he adds, still in a teasing tone, "there, ahead of you, is the Total intersection. And on the other side is the Mini Ferme intersection. Your Passe-Passe bar must be somewhere around here. Just ask and someone will direct you." Simon pays the fare and we get out. As he starts up the engine, the driver says: "Have fun, boys! You only live once!"

The place is so noisy I wonder how the locals can sleep. The bars, filled mainly with very young kids, are pumping out the latest hits at an ear-splitting level. Some are dancing on the terraces, their movements very suggestive of making love. I can't tell the difference between the girls here on a night out and the professionals. The panthers, in their Lady Gaga heels and ultra-mini, figure-hugging dresses, nearly all look like tarts.

Some of them accost us. Simon even lets them put their hands on his trousers, which surprises me a little. But I must say that some of them are wearing such low-cut tops that they'd do better to bare their little lemons or their huge watermelons altogether. "Come on honey, shall we go?" "Hey lover boy, with me it's satisfaction or your money back!" "Hey boys, don't listen to those matchsticks! Come to Ma Tempur if you want a nice soft mattress!"

So much noise, against the hum of the generators supplying the hundreds of bars in the area.

Suya vendors are doing a roaring trade with their meat skewers. Chicken, pork and grilled-fish sellers stand outside the bars, to the drunkards' delight. There are street vendors hawking everything from kola nuts to bananas, ginger, bitter kola, ginseng root and other barks that guarantee you a nice, hard *plantain*. They also sell cigarettes-sweets-chewing-gum-condoms. When I was younger, Ma used to say to Sita Bwanga that the condoms they sold by the roadside were past their sell-by date and, worst of all, they were too small. "You'd think they were made by the Chinese."

Simon and I spot a gorgeous specimen standing on a corner, a little aloof. She has long legs and a tight little ass in a fuchsia-pink synthetic dress. Simon thinks she's pretty hot. Since when was he interested in tarts? "Let's go and talk to her," he says.

"Are you going to pay for pussy?"

"Who said I was going to screw her?"

"I was just asking."

"I've got a feeling she knows where the Passe-Passe is."

"Yeah, yeah, right . . ."

"Bah . . . if we don't ask anyone, there's no point sticking around here, is there? We may as well go back to Douala."

Once level with the girl, Simon gives a friendly "hi." She turns around and smiles. *I swear!* She's really beautiful! Her blond wig looks totally natural. Ebony blonde: quite rare for that kind of wig to look good on girls, but in her case – how can I put it? – it rocks! She looks like Beyoncé, but darker. The ebony blonde is tall and slim – a supermodel. Her high heels make her even taller. Her teeth are well looked-after, as white and regular as the keys on a piano. Simon devours her with his eyes. Next to him, more surprised than aroused, I feel sort of embarrassed. "We're looking for the Passe-Passe bar. Do you know it, *chérie coco*?" ventures Simon.

"Are you footballers, too, is that it?"

The young woman's deep voice leaves no room for doubt. She's actually a he. A bucket of cold water, I imagine, for Simon. He stands there tongue-tied, taking in the tranny's features one by one. Not at all disconcerted, the blonde carries on smiling at us and says: "Come, my sweeties!" adding in an even deeper voice, "Shall we go? I'll show you sixty-ninth heaven. With me, it's all-in-one. What's more, I've got a master's in fellatio."

Simon's uncomfortable, and, suppressing my laughter, I check that no one's watching us. But it's the opposite: our tranny's leggy rivals are waiting for us to say no before rushing over. Simon gives a forced smile. A slightly wry smile. But the tranny's a pro. "You've got such beautiful eyes, my darling, all you need to do is choose your positions! Just tell me your religion, and I'll look after the rest."

"My religion?" asks Simon.

"For fuck's sake, it's obvious! For Catholics, the missionary. For Muslims, doggy style. Believe me, I'm highly experienced, baby."

Simon says nothing, particularly as the ebony blonde tranny offers him a monthly subscription at a discount:

"Only for you, darling! A special rate."

"We'll see about that later," Simon eventually says, deeply embarrassed, but revived by the bottle of cold water I've just given him. "Right now, I'm looking for the Passe-Passe. Once I've finished what I have to do there, I'll come back and see you . . ."

"Oh sweetheart! I'm not stupid! We hardly know each other and you're already lying to me as if we'd been married for ten years. Ooh là là! That's really cute. I love it!"

I can't help letting out a snort. I can't resist saying something idiotic: "Oh Roger! Thanks to you, Simon, our Simon, has found a soulmate. Oh, you're good, Roger! You're really good!"

But Simon's not the sort of guy to let himself be swayed. As upright as a lamp post in front of the blonde, he draws himself up to his full height and asks: "Do you know where the Passe-Passe is, yes or no?"

The tranny lights a cigarette: "All right, okay . . ."

"You two really get on my tits! The Passe-Passe is across the street. You see? Over there, where that big Merc is parked: that's Omar's car. Make sure you don't scratch it. The boss doesn't like that. I know you want to meet him, I saw it right away. All those who want boza come and see Omar. It pisses me off! Good-looking guys like you drop a beautiful gazelle to fill the pockets of that bastard. You'll see, your Omar, he's the ugliest fucker! Even if he offered me millions, I'd never give him my ass, the fat pig."

"Benghazi Omar?"

"Omar shitface, yeah! Go and kiss his ass from me. And then come back . . . I'll give you much more to remember than that bastard. Oh sweetheart! You know, they say it's better to have a good time with Marilyn Monroe than to kick a ball in Mbeng."

At those words, Simon grabs the tranny. An inexplicable impulse. And when he lets go, he brings up a photo of Roger on his phone. "You know him, don't you? I'm sure you know him."

"What difference would that make?" asks the tranny in a voice that's both petulant and amused. "You don't want to fuck me, but you want me to give you information. Sad bastard."

Simon slips a two-thousand-franc note into the tranny's bra. "I don't give a fuck about your dough," the blonde beauty replies, without handing back the money.

"So what do you want?"

"Your plantain, asshole! I want both of your plantains. I like double acts . . ."

"What?"

"Mmm! Don't worry, baby, it'll all be fine. I told you I've got a master's in fel—"

"Okay. Okay. I get it."

Some nearby bitches snigger. They must be finding it funny, seeing Simon bargain with the long-legged creature.

"Four thousand francs, is that enough? Five thousand?" And he stuffs more money into the tranny's bra.

"All right, all right, I saw him around here a few days ago."

"Where exactly? How long ago?"

"*Ekié!* Are you a cop or what?"

"Spit it out for fuck's sake, so we can be done!"

"Okay. So, your man's called Joker."

"Joker?"

"Yes. He was Omar's Joker. He spent a bit more than a week here. Two weeks maybe. He was Omar's right-hand man. When *it* has to be moved, or moved by the girls, you need a man who can be trusted, a tough guy."

"And?"

"Well, the guy in your photo is a very nice boy. And then, within a few days, he was made Joker."

Simon keeps on. "And Joker helped move what exactly?"

"Are you a virgin, sweetheart? What kind of question is that?"

"What?"

"Do you want me to suck you to help you understand?"

"Okay. Right, that's enough. What about Joker? Where is he?"

"How would I know! He's been *go* for more than a week now."

"But where?"

"How the fuck do I know! You've got to be a virgin. Or you've gone deaf from jerking yourself off. I just told you, he's *go*."

Simon stuffs one last note between the sponge fake breasts. The tranny isn't simpering any more. "It's strange what happened to your friend. He was absolutely determined to play for Real Madrid, FC Barcelona and all that razzmatazz. He's not the only one with crazy dreams, there are more every week. But him . . . Omar corrupted him. You want boza, too, don't you?"

"No. I don't want to *go* to Mbeng."

"Do you want to be Joker?"

"That's none of your business."

"Okay, okay! It's none of my business. I'll shut up. You can just fuck off out of here. Go and see your gross pig Omar. Do what Joker did. He was a good-looking kid and I even offered to sing on his mic for free . . . You know darling . . . I give good head . . . but he said no. He preferred the White Queen, that filthy little albino bitch."

"Ah!"

"Basta! *I'm putting a G-string over my mouth.* Ask Omar about the rest. I'd better shut up. Whatever you do, don't tell him the Gazelle of Melen sent you, I don't want him on my back. Okay?"

"The Gazelle of Melen?"

"Shhhh!"

And then the tranny walks off, saying to Simon: "You won't regret it, I promise you." Simon smiles. It's as if a barrier has come down between them. He suddenly seems so at ease with this tranny that he's no longer paying any attention to me. He catches up with her and asks for her number. "I'm the Gazelle of Melen."

"And I'm Enrico," says Simon. "And that's my brother Norbert, over there."

13

A waitress with a waxy black complexion sends us over to him. "Hey Omar! There are two dudes here who want to talk to you."

He's sitting on the terrace, with two other guys. They're drinking Castels. I'm surprised: Benghazi Omar looks nothing like the fat pig described by the Gazelle of Melen. On the contrary, he's a good-looking, sporty type in his thirties. Dreadlocks cascade onto his shoulders. He's wearing Destroy jeans and a sleeveless T-shirt. He doesn't look like the powerful guru I'd imagined: a pervert surrounded by voluptuous, naked girls lolling in a swimming pool filled with champagne.

"Would you like a drink?"

"A Castel," replies Simon after a second's hesitation. "What about you?"

"The same."

We sit down. Omar asks the waitress to bring us five bottles of Castel. The other two guys stand up. They've got to run, they have an appointment. Omar insists. Again, they politely refuse. They were probably there to ask about the boza route.

After us, there will doubtless be others.

"Everything okay?" inquires Omar, smiling. He must have clocked our surprise.

"Yes, yes," says Simon. He adds: "I'm Enrico. This is my bro Norbert."

"I don't give a fuck about your bullshit tags, man. Around here, *I'm* the one who gives people names."

We look at our feet and say nothing. Simon takes a sip of nice, cold Castel. I do the same. I can feel Omar's gaze on us. Outwardly, Simon looks calm, but I'm quaking inside, even though there's nothing menacing about Omar, other than his gaze, his silence. And his nickname: Benghazi Omar. Benghazi! Oh God! I've heard so much in the media about that Libyan city . . .

Omar kicks off, calm and direct: "How much do you have for boza?" "Um . . . um . . ." Simon hesitates. "How much do we need?"

Benghazi Omar gives a mean laugh. I need a pee. I watch Simon struggling to drink his beer. Omar regains his composure. He knew from the start that we weren't boza candidates. We didn't "have the faces of real-real *strikers*, the faces of those who are prepared to do anything in order to *go*." And besides, the White Queen has told him about our little game.

"Oh, the White Queen," exclaims Simon.

"Don't try any clever stuff with Omar, my friend. Got it?"

"Very sorry, big brother," replies Simon, bowing his head.

"The White Queen is the waitress you saw earlier."

"But . . . ," says Simon, baffled. "I thought she was albino."

"Where did you get that nonsense from?"

"Um . . . I mean . . ."

"You've barely arrived on my turf and already you're chasing trannies? That does not bode well."

Silence.

I drain my bottle. Omar downs his in one. He needs to go to the toilet. "You know, guys, with beer, you drink, you piss!" He smiles, then is swallowed up by the crowd on the terrace.

Simon's sweating like after a marathon. We look at each other for a few seconds and then we both dissolve in a fit of uncontrollable giggles. Giggles of fear, of relief, of false courage. How much longer will it go on?

We don't know what kind of crook we're dealing with. It is impossible to say whether Benghazi Omar is dangerous. Simon thinks he's a regular guy. I reply that it's not exactly innocent to incite people to boza. "Has he forced anyone?" insists Simon. "Guys come because they need his help, that's all."

"His help?"

"Well I don't think he forces anyone."

We stop talking. We can't let Omar catch us discussing him. He won't like that. He'll accuse us of taking advantage of his pee-break to plot against him. And who knows, maybe he's put a mic under the table? He must be the sort of guy who wants to control everything. I say so to Simon, who says I'm being paranoid. Benghazi

Omar is too powerful to be afraid of two little midges. I should just shut up and let him, Simon, handle things. You have to know how to conduct yourself when you're negotiating with someone of his stature. He's bound to be a Gaddafi – a guide.

My fear is that Omar and his gang will abduct us, like Boko Haram with the vice-prime minister's wife. I confide my anxieties to Simon: "Best we get out while he's not here."

"Little Johnny, until proof to the contrary, we're in Cameroon, not in an American TV series, right?"

I don't feel comfortable in this world, despite the pounding music and the party atmosphere. *J'ai envie de . . . j'ai envie de faire!* Skimpily dressed women get their asses pinched and ask for more. They let punters buy them cocktails and, along with all the guys, watch a young woman who, at brief intervals, clambers onto a chair and rotates her buttocks like the blades of a ceiling fan. It's all too suggestive. A guy yells to a girl that her buttocks are like suicide bombs. Others are quieter, dozing in front of a Champions League match. A mama as fat as a cassava *bobolo* has just offered us pork skewers: "I myself, Sita Fridolo, made them with my own hands, my son. If you take five, you can have an extra two for free. A free gift!" Simon shakes his head and the woman gets annoyed: "Look at these two, with faces like that they look like a flat-screen TV! I can see you've never tasted Sita Fridolo's VIP skewers. That's your loss!"

We spot Omar in the crowd. He's making his way over to us. People all sucking up to him, greeting him with:

"Oh great Omar!" or "Oh the great Guide of Benghazi! May the Good Lord watch over you!"

He sits down once more, facing us. My fear ramps up a notch. Fuck! I desperately need a pee. Simon kicks me under the table.

"Here, I gave him the nickname Joker," begins Omar. But how does he know we've come asking for him? "Your brother is a real man. When we say guy, it's people like him we're talking about. Not losers like some!" He lights a cigarette, holds it between thumb and forefinger and continues: "The minute I saw him, I could see that he was cast-iron. A *nguigna*, a *mola*. A guy you can work with, no problem. Joker is a general. He very quickly established himself as prime minister in my government. Yeah, man! Now he's someone 'who's got balls,' as they say. It's obvious who are the *mougous*, the softies who hang out with bumboy trannies."

Simon and I are dumbstruck. My need to pee is more and more urgent. I sweat and squeeze my legs together. *I swear!* I'm going to piss my pants like a kid.

Without excusing myself, I jump up and rush to the toilet.

When I get back, I hear Omar saying: "If it had been up to me alone, man, he could have stayed here as long as he pleased. And had everything he wanted. And I mean *everything*! Big bucks, luxury cars, *ngas* with beautiful asses, a place to live, the works. Hey! Listen up guys, look at my face, prime minister in my government? That's no small thing, guys! I say *that's no small thing!*

But, well . . . He made his choice. Football's his *life*. There you are! That's how it is. What can I do?"

"He's a fan of Roger Milla," I say.

"Yeah, right," says Omar, giving me a withering look. "In any case, I hope he makes it. Because this boza you kids have heard people talking about . . . you have to be very tough to make it."

"Has he already left Cameroon?" Simon asks, this time much more composed.

"Perhaps. I don't know, man. That's not my job. My work is to show the way and give useful contacts. The rest isn't my shit. Anyhow, if he works the way he did for me, I'm not worried about him. He'll get to Mbeng all right. I bet we'll see him on TV one day, happily kicking his ball."

"But where is he now?"

"I said I don't know. Are you deaf?"

"Can he be contacted? A telephone number?"

"Who do you think you are? Are you *mbéré*, eh, are you a cop? If I say I don't know, it's because *I don't know*. Fuck!"

I entreat the Lord to sew up Simon's lips.

Luckily the waitress comes rushing over, looking panicked. She whispers something in Omar's ear. He sighs. A guy built like a tank turns up. Omar's bodyguard most likely. On his feet, he leans over to Simon, blows smoke in his face and says: "You're lucky, man. You're not bad. Try a bit harder and you could be a real man." Simon looks him straight in the eye. I knew he was brave, but now I'm really in awe. "Your brother must still be in the country. You can't just cross the border like that. Boza means having patience. Little by little. Step by step. But because Joker's strong, he's flying. He's a star, guys. He went a few days ago. He's on his way to Nigeria. Ngaoundéré, Garoua, Maroua. Do you get it, *spaz*? You wait, you calculate. With a bit of luck and some cash, you cross the border and you're in *Naija*. It can be quick, or it can be slow. Very slow even. You have to be tough. Go on, good luck, kids!"

Omar makes his way toward the big black Mercedes. His bodyguard-driver opens the rear door. They have difficulty getting through the dense traffic that keeps stopping and starting.

The waitress comes over immediately and asks if we've got our ID cards on us. Surprise! Simon keeps calm and answers yes. "You're the White Queen, aren't you? So you know where Roger is?" "The last stage of boza is Mokolo," is all she says. Then she makes a dash for the bar. The cops are here: "ID checks on everyone!" Panic. Several guys try to leave. Too late, we're surrounded.

14

When I find Simon, he's tapping on his phone. Sita Mpondo tried to call us. We didn't hear it ring.

"And now, she's not answering?"

"No."

"She leaves three messages and then doesn't answer when we call back? Odd, isn't it . . . ?"

"I'm not calling Sita Mpondo, little bro."

"What? So who are you calling, then?"

"That tall blonde. The Gazelle. Wanna know if she left me a fake number."

"The Gazelle!? You mean the tranny? That's seriously nuts! You're not thinking of our mothers but about that drag queen. You're losing it . . ."

"Uh, oh! Calm down, Johnny. Cool it, okay?"

We get into a crappy old taxi that dates back to the German presence in Cameroon. The springs in the seats dig into our bums, which makes us laugh, at the expense of the driver: his car must be his only possession. He ignores us and turns up the volume of his car radio, 102 FM: Radio Kongossa. *Women speak*: a phone-in program for housewives all over the country. The big issue this evening is mixed marriage. The listeners are divided. One argues with a strong English accent that love is color-blind and has no borders: "*no bordas*" she says. Another is outraged that women should give their *piment* to a man who's never heard of the Kingdom of Bamum or the leader Um Nyobè: "What's the world coming to?" A third, her voice tired, says she'll do anything to marry her daughter to a White man. "A *real* White man, I say. Unless you find me a rich Cameroonian . . . ," she adds, laughing. The presenter tries to reframe the discussion by arguing that love should be the most important consideration. "Love?" snorts a caller, whose shrill voice is ear-splitting. "Can you eat love, madame? I see you live comfortably there in your radio world. But let me tell you a home truth: the White man is money. Let's not pretend. Take me: I fight like an animal to keep my little business going and it earns me peanuts. Life here is hard! At the end of the month, I count out the money for the rent, the electricity and the water, which we don't even see, the children's food, the telephone, the cable TV, *Ekié!*" She gives a long sigh. The presenter tries to interrupt her, but she won't be stopped: "No, madame! Let me speak. Did I say I'd finished? . . . I was explaining that with all those outgoings, if my fifteen-year-old daughter brings home a White man as bald as her great-grandfather, of course I'm going to accept him!" The presenter can't believe her ears. Beep. Beep. Beeep.

But neither Simon nor I pay attention to the rest of the program. The air is much cooler than in Douala. Simon fumbles for the handle to wind up the window and turns to the driver, who simply shrugs. He switches from one frequency to another. Nothing but Christian stations. *Give your lives to God, Jesus will soon return.* And traditional music, too – a mix of the mvet, balafon and tam-tam; you'd think we were among the Baka Pygmies. The driver stops at a newsflash: there's just been a terrorist attack on a village in the Kolofata region, in the far north of the country. Result: eight dead and twenty or so injured, some of them severely. The nearest health center is overwhelmed. The nurses don't know which way to turn. They lack water, fresh blood sachets, everything.

A man with a strong Maghida accent gives an eye-witness account. They were sitting there, he and his friends, on mats, drinking tea, when there was an explosion a few meters away. Panic-stricken, they took refuge in their brother-host's hut. Some stayed there, prostrate, praying, surah after surah. Others eventually came out of that shack to go and help the wounded at the scene of the explosion. Pools of blood, he says. I'm struck by this expression. Perhaps because I've never experienced an attack from the inside. Now I imagine the sandy lands of the north as clay-red, like those of the south, in the Beti or Bamileke areas. The witness describes bits of brain and guts scattered in the dust. He says: "It's butcherrrry here."

The driver, who remains unperturbed – probably because he is so used to news of attacks – starts twiddling the knob again. He must be hoping to go back to the Radio Kongossa frequency. No luck. He only picks up a load of jabbering and endless sermons about the glory of God. We learn the next day via social media that Radio

Kongossa has lost its broadcasting license because it mentioned the attack. Several journalists were even sent to prison for high treason, they say.

We meet up with Sita Mpondo in Olembe. Her face a mask of worry. We tell her about our visit to Mini Ferme Melen and the latest news, including the attack.

Sita Mpondo is wearing a hairnet over her tight Afro. She deftly reties her colorful, faded pagne around her chest. She looks at us each in turn, Simon and then me. A lengthy silence. At last she says, "My son, given the circumstances, *better* you go back to Douala. It's hard for us that Roger's gone, uhmmn, but I don't want to lose you two, as well. It's too dangerous to continue the search in the north. It's tough enough in Yaounde, but up there it's worse, you'll end up in Maghida territory, where on every street corner God's bombs will send you straight to hell. *I swear!* Leave things as they are. Go home to your mothers in Douala. Go. They're praying tirelessly. And when they stop praying, do you know what they do? They telephone me. They need reassurance. My word! May the fingers of both my hands and even my tongue be chopped off if something happens to you and it's my fault. No, oh! Me, I don't want any problems!" Simon and I keep our heads bowed.

We're big boys, yes, but for her, we're still babies. Respect is nonnegotiable. Especially given her serious tone. But to my great surprise, Simon dares to answer back. "Auntie, I agree with you. The north may be dangerous. But are we going to twiddle our thumbs and wait for the Good Lord to bring Roger back to us? I think we have to carry on looking for him. We were given some reliable information this evening. We're on his trail, do you understand? *Better* we keep going to the end. And if we don't get anywhere within one or two weeks, then we'll go back to Douala."

"What if you don't come back? If . . ."

"Auntie, the bombs know when to fall."

"Eh?"

"We're not going to provoke those fanatics. The bombs know who to target. We're just looking for our brother."

"Oh Simon! Tell me you're joking. You believe the bombs don't kill innocent people . . . !"

"If Jean wants to go home, let him. But I'm carrying on. I'm going to call my mother and tell her I'm taking the night train to Ngaoundéré. Once I've explained what I'm doing, she'll understand. I hope she'll understand."

Sita Mpondo is left openmouthed, completely baffled. She was certain that her words would convince us. Honestly, today's children insist on doing things their way! She doesn't say another word but stands up and drags herself toward the bedroom. Not even a "Good night." Nothing.

Simon looks at me: "Are you coming?" What a question! To refuse would be an admission of cowardice.

And I'd be just his mother's little Choupi-Choupinours. Not a worthy son of the Moussima Bobés, and, besides, what would people say in Beedi, in Bonamoussadi and everywhere else? Roger's friend clearly loved him more than his own flesh-and-blood brother...

15

When he rings off from his long conversation with his mother, Simon sits on the end of the bed to comfort me.

He looks apologetic but determined.

His mother, Sita Bwanga, has just given him permission to take the next night train to Ngaoundéré. He taps me gently on the back of my neck. Then, with his forefinger, he strokes my chin. I look up but avoid his gaze, which is so profound, so somber, despite the bright light. Because he saw me crying, he simply says: "Come on, Johnny!" Then he lies down on the bed, pulling a pagne-cover over his thin, hairy legs.

Within minutes, he's asleep. I can hear him snoring.

I turn out my light, too, and stretch out. My eyes closed, I try to get to sleep. Impossible. Not that Simon's snoring bothers me. No. Everything about him, even his snoring, is reassuring. But now I'm thinking about Roger. I picture him the day I failed to score against the Desert Marabouts.

He was so annoyed, that evening, that when we got home, he gave me hell: *mougou*, *gaou*, wimp, idiot, clumsy oaf, pussy. He called me every monkey name. He said: "Even a little girl tap-dancer could have pulled off that *mboundja*. Oh, Jean, you cover my body with shame! The humiliation of it!"

I had burst into tears. Both because Roger had put our brother-from-another-mother, Simon, on the subs' bench, and because my toe hurt. We'd lost the opening match to much less formidable opponents. Oh my God! Before the match, the whole of Beedi was saying: "Oh, ditch the game! The Indomitable Eagles against the Desert Marabouts, it's a shoo-in, like a match between Cameroon and Mauritania."

But I was also crying because Roger was angry. He knew I was nowhere near as good as him at football. At football or at any other sport. I fully deserved my reputation as a waste of space, a clumsy idiot. Roger, on the other hand, played both basketball and volleyball like a god. He wasn't interested in handball (that was for girls), but he practiced several martial arts, particularly karate. He insisted that it was to protect me, as I was a pretty puny boy, I admit. Unable to be his henchman or his teammate, I was simply his brother. I was even more frustrated than him about it, but I don't know whether he knew that.

When Ma came home from church and found me in that state, she exploded. Seeing my injured toe, she yelled: "Who did that to you my Choupinours? Who hurt you?"

"No one."

"What do you mean, 'no one'? Your toe's been torn off and you say it's the Holy Ghost that did it? Eh, Choupi?"

She was in tears herself and shaking me.

"Tell me, my Choupi, what happened?"

"It's Roger, Ma, it's Roger."

My mother leapt up, whisked off the leather belt she was wearing and ran at my brother. Seeing her rush at him like a madwoman, he'd tried to explain how the toenail came to be torn off. Too late. When Ma loses it, nothing can halt her fury. She must have hit Roger with all her strength. She often did, but this was the first time I'd seen her attack him with such frenzy. "Do you want to kill my child? Eh?! Is that it! You want to kill my son?! You vampire! Satan himself! In the name of Jesus, you'll be defeated!"

And I tried, yes, I did, I swear, I tried to stop the onslaught by tugging at Ma's jeans. "No Ma! No Ma! He didn't do anything, Ma."

"Do you want to kill my son?! You villain! Satan! Lucifer!"

"He didn't do anything, Ma!"

But the more I pressed my hands together and implored her, the more violently she went for Roger, my Roger Milla.

Before that day, when Ma started to beat Roger, he'd always beg her forgiveness, promising never to do it again and even trying to dodge the blows. She'd got into the habit of beating him for the slightest thing. A broken glass, and it was a thrashing. A stained school uniform earned him at least a dozen slaps. If he got home late, after eight p.m., again he got a thrashing.

Now Roger liked the youth matinées – a kind of disco – that were held every Wednesday afternoon at the Byblos club in the center of Akwa. After class and after his intense sporting activities, he'd go straight to the Byblos with his friends. An opportunity, too, for him to get it on with a girl; he had lots of admirers. At first, he'd come home to Beedi no later than seven o'clock. Ma was already waiting to whip him. He was resigned to it. The harder she beat him, the later he came back the next day. Eventually, he no longer came home at all.

This time, Roger had again allowed himself to be beaten like a thief caught red-handed by the neighbors. Without a sound, he curled up in a fetal position. And when Ma stopped hitting him, he looked up and defied her with his gaze, like a boxer. It was as if he wanted to make her understand that she could beat him as much as she liked, she wouldn't get anything out of him, ever, not even his tears. Ma was hopping mad: "And he looks me in the eye! He has no respect, this boy! Evil child! Satan! You dare look at me when I'm talking to you? Gentle Jesus! Save your poor servant. I'm going to have a word with your father. Enough's enough! Either he's the master of this house and he disciplines you as he should, or I'll take care of it myself."

The ordeal only ended with Pa's arrival. Taken aback at the violence of the scene, he yelled at Ma: "Oh Ngonda! Oh Ngonda! What's the matter! Are you trying to kill Roger?"

"Aaah!" howled Ma, sweating. "So that's it . . . Now I understand everything."

"But how can you do that to your own son, eh Ngonda?"

"I tell you I've understood everything. So it's you, Claude Moussima! It's you who's turning this child against me, who stuffs his head with these wicked ideas, that he has to kill us, *my* Choupi and me. Oh yes, yes, it's all clear now. Pastor Njoh Solo was right. But that's not how things are going to go in this house. The Lord can't be good and allow you to do that! Never!"

Pa sent Roger to have a shower and then to bed. What else could he do? The pastor's word counted for more than his.

Ma didn't give Roger any food that evening, but she stuffed me with groundnut soup and rice.

Still today, that memory sears my guts. I wish I could forget it. I simply can't think of Ma as a monster. Why such a fit of rage? She was so tired that evening. She was . . . I pull another pagne-cover over my shoulders. In his sleep, Simon puts his arm around me.

I dry my tears and doze off.

16

It must be midday when I'm woken by the sound of Simon and Sita Mpondo's voices. They're talking about the night journey to Ngaoundéré and are pleased they managed to buy last-minute tickets. "Sleeper tickets, too!" says Sita Mpondo, delighted. "The train line from Yaounde to Ngaoundéré is so popular that you have to book tickets at least two days ahead to be sure of a seat. But there's no such word as impossible. You just have to add a little tip, and there you are, you're good to go."

Sita Mpondo gives a few final words of advice to Simon, who begs her not to keep on at him: of course, he won't let his wallet stick out of his trouser pocket or leave his backpack open.

I look about me. The room is similar to my bedroom at home in Bonamoussadi. Except that there are no posters of Roger Milla, and certainly not our national team. The same room, yes, but minus the damp smell of Roger's sports shirts and football boots. Minus the bunk bed, too: Sita Mpondo never had children. Ma says it'll happen one day. Sarah, in the Bible, still managed to give birth to Isaac at the age of ninety. So, no need to panic. God does as He sees fit. If He hasn't given Sita Mpondo any children, He alone knows why and we're not going to bother Him about that.

It's barely two days since we left Douala, but I'm missing my desk table. That's where I sat every night and recited Psalm 23 before going to bed. *The Lord is my shepherd, I shall not want.* Not long ago, seated there, I wondered whether I'd pass my first university exams, whether Simon's advice would help me sail through them, like him. "By the grace of God," Ma always said.

I miss her, too. On the phone, she sounds frail, even after she's recognized my voice. She's probably been crying a lot. I have no news for her, just a few words. She's happy to hear me. I end the call telling her about the Gazelle of Melen. "It's because of monsters like that that the Good Lord destroyed Sodom and Gomorrah," she says. Ma's convinced that God wanted to test our faith by putting a Gazelle with a pointed tail in our path.

Otherwise, Ma's life hasn't changed much. I know it inside out. She spends hours in a new Pentecostal Church; she left the Church of the True Gospel after Pa's death. Jesus! How many times did she take me there: she absolutely had to save me from the web of evil that she saw in Roger. On Tuesdays, she made me go to Bible study classes. Pastor Njoh Solo taught us to perform miracles, for example by transforming the waters of our anxieties into laughter. And on Friday evenings, I wasn't allowed to watch my favorite telenovela: *The Triumph of Love.*

I had to attend the Sisters in Christ gatherings. They'd sit in a circle, like at Alcoholics Anonymous meetings in American soaps. I remember one time, when one of the sisters had complained of a husband who both cheated on her and beat her, who wanted to throw her out. The pastor's wife said to her confidently, before inviting the group to pray in a sort of language specific to those who have received the Holy Ghost:

"All things work together for the good of those who love God."

In her prayers, Ma has ever only wished for two things. And while God had quickly granted the first – Pa had bought a house – He was refusing to grant the second: Roger didn't change. Pastor Njoh Solo thought the devil had got into my brother's heart. And so he had to be freed.

One Friday, during the meeting, Ma had begun sobbing as she told the sisters about her woes with Roger. He'd just been expelled from the Conquête du Savoir school, after getting a girl in his class, Sylvie Mbarga, pregnant. The girl's mother had come racing round to our house. I can still see her, holding her daughter firmly in one hand, and in the other, a bundle that must have contained her belongings. Ma was shimmying to the rhythm of old Makossa songs, the sounds of her youth. She reckoned that those Makossas would even have got the Holy Father wiggling his hips. It was very bad timing. Sylvie Mbarga's mother was in no mood to shake her bootie with Ma. "Hey, you madame! Yes, I'm talking to you! Instead of teaching your son how to behave, you're dancing, so that's how it is?"

"Yes, I'm dancing. And who are you?"

"Me, I'm the mother of the girl your son has made pregnant."

"And who told you it was my son who swelled her belly? A well-brought-up girl keeps her legs closed: didn't you teach her that at least?"

"Like mother, like son," the woman replied, livid. "You shameful woman! You minx!"

In front of her Sisters in Christ, Ma had been careful not to mention that she had jumped on Sylvie Mbarga's mother, had hit her and ripped her dress. And of course, not a word either about the thrashing she'd immediately given Roger.

Sylvie Mbarga's abortion, a few weeks later, had been somewhat of a relief for her.

In short, Ma prays morning, noon and evening. Nonstop. Like a real sentry, the Bible as her sword, she fights the evil spirit wherever she senses it. Having received proof that God had granted her first wish, she clung hard to the second. She clung so hard to it that she ended up spending a fortune. "Give and you will receive": That's how Pastor Njoh Solo spoke. And Ma had given. Oh, had she given – wads of notes for the collection and the tithe! She was so obsessed by her troubles with Roger that she always had to slip a little something into God's hand so that He'd put her top of His priorities. Thanks to all her giving, Ma had been made deaconess. The pastor said he'd received the order from God: "My servant Njoh Solo, take my daughter Ngonda Moussima Bobé as deaconess in my temple."

When Pa found out that Ma was giving so much cash to the church, he got angry and ordered her not to spend any more on "those sects." And Ma replied that the donations didn't go into the pastor's pocket, as he thought, but directly to heaven. Pa roared with laughter. Bitter laughter. "My wife, Ngonda! Oh, my poor wife! Heaven . . . but where on earth did you get such nonsense? Your pastor simply takes the money that you and the other fools give him. He throws it up in the air, perhaps intending God to help Himself to it, hup la! But he picks up all the money that falls back down. That's how it works, you stupid woman!"

Now that Pa's dead, I don't think she has enough money to pay the tithe or contribute to the collection: that must break her heart.

On the telephone, earlier, I promised Ma I'd be good. I assured her I'd recite Psalm 23 at least five times a day. She said "Amen" and then rang off.

Roger is in Maroua, according to Simon. He's just told me. "Did you manage to get hold of him? Who told you he's there?" His informer, apparently, is the Gazelle of Melen. Oh God! That tranny again! Simon must have made contact that morning. And because he knows I don't trust that cock-sucking queen one bit, he adds: "I also talked to the White Queen, on Facebook. She's unblocked me." So apparently Roger's in Maroua staying with El Hadj Bassirou for a few more days. El Hadj Bassirou is the spiritual son of Benghazi Omar. He's the last Cameroonian you see before crossing over into Nigeria.

17

Sita Mpondo drives us to Yaounde railway station, in the heart of the teeming Elig Essono neighborhood. When we arrive in her little red Toyota Starlet, we're surprised to see a dense crowd at the security barrier. "What's going on here?" exclaims our auntie in annoyance. "I hope they haven't had the bright idea of holding an evangelization drive here." She mutters criticism of the authorities who allow Pentecostal churches to spring up here like weeds. She struggles to park in the undergrowth in front of one of the station's many tourne-dos. The owner yells at her: "Hey, madame! *Madame!* Do you expect people to go through your car to get to my eatery, eh?"

"My brother," Sita Mpondo replies, bowing her head in childlike entreaty, "I'm simply going to take my sons here into the station and I'll be back quick-quick to remove my car."

The restaurant guy backs off, but threatens to have our auntie's car towed away if she doesn't move it within an hour. Sita Mpondo mutters: "And has he got a sales license? Has he got a permit? He'd better not annoy decent, upstanding citizens like us."

We don't understand the reason for this gathering in front of the station any more than Sita Mpondo does.

She often comes to this area, but she's never seen such a crowd. In front of us, a lady with buttocks as heavy as her enormous suitcases explains that the military have imposed routine searches of all travelers across the entire country. It's been like this since early morning.

"Eh?" asks Sita Mpondo in surprise. "Why? Haven't they got anything better to do?"

"It's because of Boko Haram, my sister." The lady whispers, as if the weight of her buttocks has crushed her voice. "They say that Boko Haram is everywhere. That even little-little girls with the sheet over their heads can come here and Boko-Haramize us."

Luckily, at Simon's insistence, we'd set out in good time for our first railway journey. He was afraid of missing the train.

Simon checks his smartphone and confirms: in response to the attacks by the Allah fanatics, our Papa-President's government has decided not only to ban the full-length veil, but also to conduct general and routine searches in most public places: ministries, airports, schools, university campuses, hospitals, bars, markets, mosques, churches, bus and railway stations, and anywhere else crowds gather. An antiterrorist law would soon be put before Parliament, at the request of our Papa-President. "Ah!" cries Sita Mpondo with a mocking expression. "Even sneezing will become a terrorist act!"

A few paces away, a dozen soldiers are trying to create order in this vast human mass. A single-line queue forms, but it is still essentially Cameroonian. The lady with the heavy buttocks is jostled a great deal. She's very pleased when Simon eventually makes a little room for her in the line, where everyone is shoving her. "God bless you, my son."

On the other side of the barrier, another dozen or so officers are busy searching people. Laughing, half-surprised and half-annoyed, we discover some strange equipment: metal detectors. "What now, with these Chinese toys?" asks a man who's about to lose his rag. An outburst of laughter from the crowd. "Whatever next?!" comments Sita Mpondo.

The search seems to be more complicated for women. The inspectors say to them: "Hey you, with your big kaba ngondo, are you sure you're not hiding a bomb in there?" Or: "Are those breasts of yours real, sister? Because they look as if they're going to explode any minute."

Despite the torpor, the weariness and the wait, the mood is good-humored. People are in stitches when a woman asks if the metal detectors can tell us about the treasures hidden inside the big hair of our Papa-President's wife. A child whines. His mother threatens to shut him up in a suitcase. A young woman, on the phone, is having a go at someone: "Yes, that's it! If it was for that little tart of yours, you'd soon get your ass over here. But because it's me, monsieur doesn't have the time!"

Travelers who'd made the unfortunate choice to wear a *gandoura* are searched much more thoroughly. "You! Raise your hands!" the inspector commands a guy who must be from the north. "Are you the one bringing bombs into our country? Are you?"

"Excuse me! Excuse me! But doesn't this country belong to all of us?"

"Shut it, you sheep! Besides, what's that big thing down there?"

"What?"

"There, down there, I say."

"But that's my . . . it's my . . ."

"What?! Is that your plantain in there? Pooopopo! Step aside so we can check. Since when is that thing so long?"

Another huge wave of laughter envelops the crowd. The girls snigger as they stand on tiptoe better to see the guy with the amazing penis.

We finally get through the barrier. After we've shown our tickets and our ID, our backpacks are ripped open. Are the metal detectors working? Even though Sita Mpondo doesn't have a ticket, she *warmly greets* the inspector. He gives her a big smile, baring his yellow teeth, and immediately signals to her to move on. Our auntie doesn't even open her bag.

It's close to nine p.m. Almost three-quarters of an hour late. More lengthy hugs and we're off.

Through the window of our sleeper car, Simon and I wave back as best we can as Sita Mpondo on the platform gesticulates frantically, growing smaller and smaller as the train moves off. Let's hope she doesn't get angry with the tourne-dos owner . . .

Once again, we're alone in the world. Time is against us. "We should be in Maroua within twenty-four hours," says Simon with a calmness that doesn't conceal his anxiety.

If the Gazelle of Melen and the White Queen were speaking the truth, we mustn't lose a minute in Ngaoundéré, but take a bus to Garoua straight away. Three or four hours for that journey. Then from Garoua to Maroua, another three or four hours and that's it. Ideally, we should be at El Hadj Bassirou's door the next evening.

18

Sita Mpondo warned us not to leave our carriage for fear of being robbed. "I'm telling you, don't even leave your compartment." A female attendant knocks on the door to take our dinner orders. "We have everything we need," Simon replies. The young woman's gaze lingers on his bare chest. She gives him a knowing smile and leaves.

Simon eats *bobolo* with fried chicken; Sita Mpondo bought some the previous day from her favorite caterer. Lying on the bottom bunk, I watch Simon. Everything about him fascinates me: his chest, his abs, his face, his eyes, his lips . . . his clean-shaven chin. Still not a hair on mine.

I miss Douala! I feel as if I've left the country. Luckily, I'm with Simon: if I wasn't, I'd die of anxiety and grief. I daren't admit it: he'd laugh at me. "So what about those attempting boza, then?" he'd be bound to say playfully.

I miss Roger. My mother. My father. But not just them. Pa Bomono, our neighborhood chief in Bonamoussadi, always a glass of palm wine within reach. And the owner of the hugely popular Empereur Bokassa bar. Ah, that woman! . . . I can still see her shooing away her last customers, drunk and loudmouthed. It's possible she's never found a bra big enough to contain her enormous breasts. Her bosom is the main attraction for the men of Bonamoussadi. They've nicknamed her Miss Lolo. When Miss Lolo walks past, all the married women – even old Ma Bomono – hold on to their husbands. I've never understood why Miss Lolo chose the name "Bokassa" for her bar. One of the Nyanga Boys team told me that she'd been the mistress of a relative of the emperor of the Central African Republic, a diamond merchant. He told me that this man's money had enabled her to open her business.

Simon asks if I'm hungry. Watching him was all the nourishment I needed. I'd rather listen to old Makossa songs, especially Charlotte Mbango's *Konkaï makossa*, the one Ma listens to when she wants to pour a little joy into her heart. A pity, Simon only has R'n'B hits on his phone. But I don't like that American stuff. And besides, Pastor Njoh Solo has forbidden us to listen to that kind of music. He even told us that when you play those songs backward, you can hear the voice of Lucifer himself. "Be vigilant, my dear brothers and sisters in Christ," he concluded. "Keep your ears away from things of unbelievers."

We've brought books with us: Mongo Beti's *Cruel City* and *Agatha Moudio's Son* by Francis Bebey. Simon recommends the Boto. He wants to reread Francis Bebey, a classic from our school years. I've read passages to him loads of times for dictation practice.

He's particularly fond of *Agatha Moudio's Son* because the novel reminds him of his mother's story.

Sita Bwanga comes from a poor family. She was born and grew up in Ngodi-Akwa, in a slum dwelling that her parents had built too hastily. They'd put chunks of breezeblock on the rusty roof to hold it down when the winter winds blew. The Bwangas only ate once a day. That was the fate of the vast majority of people who lived in the area. The rest of the time, there was fruit, lots of different kinds: mangos, sugar cane, guava, bananas and many others. The young Bwanga girl had not gone far in her studies. Once she reached womanhood, she soon became an object of desire for many men. Several had come to *speak* to her parents. They announced their intention of coming to *knock on the door* to pay a bride price.

The Bwanga parents had promised their daughter to Kamga, a wealthy businessman from the west of the country. It was common knowledge that he already had two wives. So long as they lived a long way from Douala – one was in Yaounde and the other in Limbe – anything was possible. And even the little Bwanga girl consented.

Very quickly, Kamga started helping the family financially. Things moved fast. There was more and more talk of *knocking on the door* and planning the civil wedding ceremony. Particularly since the young Bwanga girl had fallen pregnant. It was wonderful. Kamga showered his future wife with a thousand gifts and honors. He had eyes only for her. Too bad for her flat-chested rivals in Yaounde and Limbe! Those two women were nothing more than squeezed lemons now.

Up until the birth, Sita Bwanga was the pride of her family. But – God help us! – her daughter was born with a skin that was far, far too light. Okay, even granted that Sita Bwanga's skin was banana-colored (which is what Kamga loved most about her), even so, this convinced no one.

The Ngodi-Akwa parliament of busybodies held an urgent meeting at the neighborhood well. They were convinced that the Bwanga girl had done an *Agatha Moudio:* she'd cheated on her husband and become pregnant by another, from a different race. "Even more shameful!" they decreed, slapping their hands and laughing. Tos-tas!

One month after the birth of Kotto – Simon's older sister – things were clearer: Kamga had been well and truly cuckolded. But no way was mother Bwanga going to allow a son-in-law as wealthy as Kamga to slip through her fingers. She decided to take things in hand. And how! She argued that there was White blood in her lineage. "For centurieeeees!" she shouted adamantly from all the rooftops of Ngodi-Akwa. Yes, that White blood had been left in the belly of one of her ancestors by the very first German colonists . . . No, by the Portuguese, who took it upon themselves to name the Wouri river *Rio dos Camarões* – Prawn River. And at a plenary session of the parliament of busybodies one deputy said: "If Ma Bwanga is White, then so is my ass!"

After a year, the evidence was plain: Kotto was not from Kamga's seed. And *sand in the sauce* – I swear on Pasteur Njoh Solo's head, she wasn't even the child of a White man – like in *Agatha Moudio's Son* by Francis Bebey. No. Little Kotto was the fruit of an Asian seed! *Bad luck!* You should have heard what people said about her slanting little eyes, her too-smooth hair and her copper-toned skin!

Kamga stormed off, furious. He threatened to ask for the presents he'd given his future wife to be returned. He called the Bwanga parents *feymen* – swindlers, cheats, thieves, sorcerers . . . He was at a loss to find enough insults to describe them!

It was Simon himself, after a dictation, who'd told me this story. I suddenly understood why his sister – whom I hadn't known very well when we lived in Beedi as kids – didn't look at all like him. Simon's father? That's another story, I imagine. All I know about him is that he was supposedly Sita Bwanga's great love. He departed very early, killed by a merciless typhoid fever.

Now Kotto lives in Paris, where she works as a super-size model . . .

When Simon tells me that his sister wants him to continue his studies in Paris, I open my eyes wide in panic. He adds that he's not like Roger, he likes being in Cameroon.

19

When I wake up, the train has stopped.

I open the window of our compartment and the night is the deepest black. I don't know where we are, or why we're there. I glance at the top couchette: Simon isn't there. Don't panic, okay? Breathe. He must have gone to the toilet. I wait for him for a few minutes. Maybe a quarter of an hour. When he's not back after twenty minutes, I start to worry. I wonder if there's a connection between his absence and the fact that the train has stopped.

In the corridor, two male voices complain that there's been no announcement for more than an hour. They also say that anti–Boko Haram commandos, en route for the Nigerian border, alighted from the train so as to guarantee our safety.

Now I really am in a panic.

Where the hell has Simon got to?

When I reach the dining car, it's packed. All the passengers appear to have made their way there. On their faces: fear and dread, but also weariness. Some are saying the train has broken down. They fume against the rolling stock, supposedly dating back to the days of Charles de Gaulle's presence in Cameroon. Others say it's simply a halt to take more supplies on board. "Nonsense!" retorts a man with a square head. "How can they stock up in the middle of the night, in the middle of the forest, without a shadow of a village nearby?"

One theory is often repeated: there might have been a Boko Haram attack! Those religious fanatics often operate by blocking roads, holding up trains, assaulting the passengers, robbing them and, above all, making them recite passages of the Qur'an by heart. And then, Allah! one little mistake and they chop off your hand. But it's never too late, because the assembled passengers ask a Maghida woman swathed in colorful pagnes to teach us one or two of the best-known verses of the Qur'an there and then. *Everything in the Heavens and the Earth Glorifies Allah. Allah is powerful and wise.* We chant that verse. I even add: *To Allah belongs all honor, power and glory . . .* One person blurts out: "And if we all recite the same verse, won't the Boko-Haramers say we must imagine they're stupid?"

"That's just what I was thinking," says an elderly man with a beard.

"In any case, *I'm* not going to start learning the Qur'an at two o'clock in the morning. I'd rather die for Yésu. At least that way I'll go to heaven. Direct!"

"Idiot! Do you really believe in all that rubbish about heaven?"

"Yes, yes. Heaven exists," adds a man who's clearly drunk, clutching his bottle of Castel. Heaven is our Papa-President's Etoudi pa-palace." The entire dining car laughs uncontrollably.

But suddenly there's the sound of gunshots. And everyone lies down on the floor. Silence. Terror. Gentle Jesus! Where is Simon? I turn my head to the left and to the right. Inwardly I recite: *The Lord is my shepherd, I shall not want.* And then I try to remember the verse from the Qur'an. Shit, shit, shit, I've already forgotten it!

Discreetly I slide my phone out of my pocket to send a warning message. Who to? Not my mother, no, no, no. She'd die if she knew her little Choupi was in a situation like this. And Sita Bwanga would want to know how her son was. Sita Mpondo maybe . . . No. She'd panic, too. She'd yell that she'd warned us of the danger. It's Simon I want to call. Oh God, where is he, my Simon?

We hear the thud of boots, a dry branch cracking. It sounds as if someone's being chased. But is it the Boko-Haramers pursuing our soldiers or our soldiers pursuing them? Let Jesus come back, for goodness' sake! Pastor Njoh Solo and his wife say that all good things come to those who love God. So, if this is my time, well, I'm ready! . . . But no! I don't want to die!

The drunkard's voice calls out to us. The fool cackles: "Don't panic! Don't panic! A presidential helicopter will come and pick us up." Some people stifle their laughter. Me, I keep my jaw clenched.

At last, there's an announcement over a loudspeaker: "Ladies and gentlemen, our train will be leaving in a few minutes. We apologize for this little inconvenience." A great "Aaah!" of discontent rises in the dining car. A woman fumes: "Fuck your mothers! Do you hear? Fuck fuck fuck your mothers! Fear is eating my belly and all you can say is 'Yada yada yada, our train will be leaving in a few minutes'? Bunch of thugs! Murderers! Terrorists! Boko-Haramers!" She's not the only one. Insults fly. Others are already glued to their phones: they must be posting the information on Facebook or trying to contact their families.

Simon still isn't answering my calls.

People applaud the soldiers when they board the train. They're sweating profusely, panting like marathon runners at the end of a race. No way of knowing what they did out there. But what strikes me is how young they are and how extremely good-looking. Perhaps we're the same age.

The women cheer and ululate. They spread their pagnes and headscarves on the floor for the soldiers to walk on, like Jesus on Palm Sunday. The soldiers smile at us and make V-signs. But what really happened out there? Under the blanket of applause, I hear people saying that they might have been chasing simple thugs who block roads, that they certainly weren't Boko Haram terrorists. *Aka!* All that fuss about nothing! According to the drunkard, our commandos simply fired into the air. "Wait! W-wait!" he shouts. "Let me tell you what really happened out there: it's our Papa-President who rescued us." More laughter, and everyone comes up with their own little theory. Everyone says they know all about terrorism. A man eventually shouts: "Come on, waiter! A cold beer for everyone? They're on me!"

The track is clear. The train starts moving again.

I go back to our compartment, and Simon is there. "Where the fuck were you, eh?" No reply. "Fuck you, you're a pain! Fucker, asshole. Fucking idiot! What the hell were you doing? I nearly wet myself waiting for you!" By way of reply, Simon lowers his head and picks up his Gideon New Testament. But I go on at him. I yank his Bible out of his hands and throw it! I will not calm down, no way. *Fuck off!* Let him talk to me, the bastard! I need him to look at me! Reassure me, say something, for fuck's sake! He has no idea how worried I was! Does he realize, name of Yésu? I cry like a baby. Simon comes over to me, puts a very gentle hand on my head, and finally puts his arms around me. "Everything's going to be all right Johnny. Okay? We've just got to pray very hard that we get to Ngaoundéré safe and sound."

20

It's one o'clock in the afternoon when we arrive. Three hours late, not to mention the time we lost at the checkpoint in Yaounde. Although the previous night's incident had left us – or at least me – with a forest of fears, we were at least relieved that our heads were still firmly on our shoulders. Simon asks me to forget what happened on the train: "The main thing is that we're alive and the two of us are together, right?"

On the platform, the waiter from the dining car yells after the passengers: "Hey! Wait! Where's the gentleman who ordered beers for an entire carriage?" No one bats an eyelid. "Ay, ay, ay, ay! The guy's run off with my money! Now what am I going to tell my boss?"

Simon distanced himself from me slightly. Actually, he hurried to catch up with the attendant who'd come to take our dinner orders the previous evening. A great rapport between the two of them, immediately. Anyone would think they'd known each other forever. I'm seething. Who is this bitch who's making him smile all over? Come on Simon, she looks like a sow. Big, fat whatever. At least the Gazelle of Melen, with her long legs, blond wig and false breasts wasn't bad. A sort of doe! But this one looks like a rotten mango. Look at her nose, for goodness' sake!

As big as a double exhaust pipe. And besides, she *uses ndjansan*, huh, she bleaches her skin. Her elbows, knees and fingers are still dark brown. Bitch! Women like that are called *fanta-coka*. Simon clearly doesn't give a shit what I think of her.

He's very happy to walk beside her. And suddenly I understand the reason for his disappearance last night. No need for him to spell it out.

They give each other a goodbye kiss. All dripping with affection. Ooh, how I'd love to strangle that girl!

After buying a phone top-up at the station, Simon calls each of our mothers in turn and reassures them. He doesn't hand the phone to me. I don't particularly want to talk to them anyway. Let the whole world leave me in peace! He tells them I'm fine. Good. I can tell he's afraid I'll tell them about our train being attacked.

Ngaoundéré bus station is right opposite the great mosque. A sweaty crowd is queueing outside. With our backpacks, Simon and I perspire like demolition workers. We elbow our way through to the front of the line at the ticket window. You have to show ID and negotiate the price depending on how much baggage you have, and, if possible, add on a little something if you'd rather not sit next to a hen or sheep destined for slaughter for the Tabaski festival. After this little performance, in theory we should be able to board the next bus leaving for Garoua. Except we can't. With our ticket numbers, we can only take the next bus or even the one after that. A motorboy is supposed to call out our names.

There's nothing for it but to be patient. Benghazi Omar warned us.

So, I slump onto one of those long, battered, backless benches they have in the waiting room. A teenage girl whose face is covered in spots is holding a snotty-nosed baby who is probably her own. She's just lifted up her cardigan to stuff one of her little breasts in its mouth. Oh God! . . . Nearby, scrawny brats, barefoot and filthy, are playing football with an avocado stone. I try to kick it back to them when it lands between my legs. Still just as rubbish at kicking a ball . . .

The call to prayer rings out from the minaret across the road: *Allahu Akbar!* The men, who are all holding jugs, must be coming back from their ablutions. All unfurl their brightly colored plastic prayer mats on the ground and make graceful, instinctive movements with their prayer beads before settling down to pray in earnest. Meanwhile, the women stand behind them, with their very colorful veils. A solemn moment.

Simon, who'd slipped away again when I wasn't looking, comes back from God-knows-where. He says it'll be a good hour before we leave. He glares at the mosque. He doesn't want to stay among people who are bowing down, kneeling and then banging their foreheads on the ground. "Let's go for a little walk. There must be some good suya around here."

There are three of us on a Hyundai motorcycle taxi. The driver's a kid barely past puberty. He rides with utter recklessness. Every so often, he lets go of the handlebars to adjust his helmet. Simon is sitting behind me. He knows I'm scared and holds me tight. Come on, we can forget the fanta-coka, my Simon is back. My knees are still trembling and the teenaged driver notices: "Are you scared?" he taunts. "Fuck it Simon, we should just get off," I say, turning my head. But getting off would also mean losing precious physical contact with him. Please God, let our ride end and not end!

The kid driver, suddenly held up in a traffic jam near the Lamido palace esplanade forces us to get down: "Make your own way, guys!"

The crowd is in celebratory mood because the turbaned horsemen are galloping full tilt on the road. Their mounts, white, black, Chinese, are decked out in multicolored frills. Men and women are dancing to the beat of traditional music.

Simon taps me on the shoulder: "We can't waste time on this folklore, come on. Let's go and find our suya and get out of here. I'm sure there's a suyaman over there."

The bus taking us to Garoua is overcrowded and the heat inside is merciless. Not even the faltering air con of Security Voyage! We're squashed together and Simon is pressed really close against me. The single mother with the snot-nosed baby is sitting in front of us. She does nothing but feed her infant. Two men complain about the conditions in which we're traveling. The driver suggests they get out and continue their journey on foot. They grumble and then shut up.

Our neighbor, a skinny guy as black as *mbongo* sauce, asks us if we're from the area. No, answers Simon. The man isn't surprised. We look more like people from the south, which he knows well. When Simon tells him we're from Douala, he goes wild with joy. "And I'm a math teacher in the New-Bell High School. I'm visiting my family."

Talking with him, we learn that even though he was on a different night train to us, he, too, had a terrifying experience: stopping in the middle of the nowhere, shots fired, panic.

The minibus slows down: a dry tree trunk is lying across the road. Soldiers saunter over to us, as if the heat has drained them of all energy. They order the passengers to get out. The makeshift barrier is then moved so that the empty bus can move forward a few meters. The driver gives the vehicle documents to the soldiers along with a generous tip, both to perk them up and speed things along. After a rapid search of the engine and the baggage compartment (they don't go so far as to check the credentials of the sheep bleating on the roof), one at a time, arms slightly raised, we let ourselves have our bodies swept by the metal detectors and show the soldiers our ID. The point of this operation seems to be to reassure us.

But we leave minus three passengers: they didn't have any ID. Simon tells me that in his view, given the down-

and-out appearance of the guys who were taken away, they most likely hadn't had on them the small sum of cash necessary to soften up the inspectors. That was their bad luck. Further on, we pick up four old men who came out of nowhere. They pay the full fare.

After two or three similar checks, Simon tells Oumarou, the math teacher, the reason for our trip. He shows him a photo of Roger on his phone. Oumarou shakes his head, very sorry: he doesn't recognize the face. He praises our courage. "I wish I'd had brothers like you boys." Even so, he reminds us of the risk we're running if we stay in the region too long. He lost two friends in Boko Haram raids in Mora and Koza, very close to the border. He says he knows lots of young women who were raped in front of the entire village, in front of their families in particular, their parents, their children. They are ruined women who can no longer hear a surah without being reminded immediately of those Allah fanatics who recited the Qur'an while fucking them. As a result, no one knows what to do with them. Even if, as they say, they have been sown with the seed of the Prophet, we don't want to marry women who are sullied. So, they end up being given to Allah's warriors. *Allahu Akbar!*

"You know, brothers," the math teacher goes on in his heavy Maghida accent, "down south, we don't hear anything about the attacks of those thugs. People drink their beer and dance as if everything's fine, whereas those madmen are advancing every day and crushing us like mosquitoes." Silence. Oumarou continues confidently:

"It's the Whites who are to blame for all this. They're trying to destabilize the country. When we're at peace, it doesn't suit them. They have to come and ruin everything."

Oumarou speaks of the boza routes. Apparently, there's also one in the southwest, which leads to Calabar, in southern Nigeria. But because militias from the Niger delta kidnap at will, boza candidates now tend to go via Mokolo, to the west of the town of Maroua. The teacher adds, his throat wobbling with mockery: "Who knows, maybe I'll go for it myself one of these days. This country's becoming too hard, brothers. Too *hard*! Look at me, I work like crazy, and I haven't been paid in three months. Nothing! I'm going to visit my family in my village, empty-handed. Do you think that's right? When we demand our salaries, the Treasury says it's released funds, but for whom? We don't see any of the money. The principal simply told us that we were free to resign if we were dissatisfied. But between you and me, brothers, in this country of ours, who's going to get up one fine morning and walk out? Who?! We're forced to stay here and put up with things. *What are we going to do?*"

Once more, the driver pulls over by the roadside. I glance out of the window: no roadblock, no soldiers. It's the pray-to-Allah break. Three-quarters of the passengers get out. They each have a prayer mat under their arm and a water bottle for their ablutions in their hand.

I take advantage of the halt to stretch my legs and buy some dates and salted groundnuts. "Oh Simon," I say, "we're not going to get to Maroua this evening, are we? It's nearly six o'clock and we haven't even reached Garoua." Simon, without a word, runs off to pee in a bush. I shout: "The Maghida here won't wait for you if you waste time, will they?"

21

When we finally reach Garoua, I wonder whether this is still Cameroon. The landscape dotted with isolated shrubs and with expanses of fine sand on the horizon is so different from the raw, intense green of the forests of the south. I can't get over it.

Darkness has already fallen. We won't have had the chance to see the hippopotamuses that are said to doze on the peaceful banks of the Benue. A light, cool wind dispels the bus's smell of adulterated petrol; in places, it raises the dust like a whirlwind.

Simon asks Oumarou for the address of a cheap place to spend the night. Oumarou offers to put us up in his village, about an hour away. But we're too exhausted to travel any further. At dawn, we absolutely have to take the first bus to Maroua because we want to arrive at El Hadj Bassirou's early. The teacher thinks for a moment. He knows the nearby Savane Rose, a hostel that's just heaven for visitors passing through. "You'll be very well looked after!" he laughs, adding: "You can even make the most of *room service*."

We head down Rue du Pont, a wide, tarmac road with lots of shops. There are illicit vendors of adulterated petrol every hundred meters, and the kids selling it call out to us: "The cheapest *zoua-zoua* here, uncles! Come and buy!" Worm-eaten wooden constructions line the sandy pavements. Convenience stalls selling cigarettes-sweets-chewing-gum. The volume of the music in the handful of bars is so low that I almost miss the deafening racket of Miss Lolo's Empereur Bokassa or Benghazi Omar's Passe-Passe. I tell myself that Ma would like it here, she'd just need a little *Konkaï makossa*.

When the call to prayer rings out, it's the same unlikely procession of believers.

The women are on the skinny side. We don't meet a single one who has the voluptuous curves of the woman at Yaounde railway station. Many of them are veiled with wide, colored pagnes that look like Indian saris. Some of them have a discreet nose piercing. I'm struck by the henna patterns of flowers covering the hands and feet of one young woman. She's carrying a baby on her back and has a scar on her right cheek.

We walk past the headquarters of the BIR, the rapid intervention brigade. Athletic young commandos stand in front of the wall and barbed wire fencing surrounding the security zone. God, they look like fierce dogs! They're not at all like the lethargic soldiers inspecting the buses and have nothing of the mocking air of the ones at Yaounde railway station. Oh Roger, my brother! See how, because of you, we're facing soldiers armed to the teeth! I'm even more scared when Simon whispers that these BIR guys only know how to kill. I imagine them checking us out behind their shades, which they wear even though it's the middle of the night. Simon smiles at my comment and asks me to be discreet. He says: "Look straight head and keep walking."

A few dozen meters further on, Simon points to a big commercial building. Good heavens: a branch of the Cameroonian national beer company! My mind is immediately inundated with memories. I think back to the first glasses of beer Pa got us to taste to save us from the Lipton-tap water, to his blackout of course, and, for a second, I even see him at the funeral, in his coffin, stiff in his ridiculous three-piece suit and handsome as a god-without-shoes.

After brilliant studies among the half-Whites of Algeria and Morocco, Pa had made his career as a brewer for the SABC, in Yaounde and then in Douala. "By the grace of God," he was made deputy production manager, *no less*. No beer bottling without his say-so. Latent inebriation was his normal state, his lucid state. Even at the wheel. Ma would say to him: "Claude! The beer you make will be the death of you, I'm telling you." When she complained, Pa would reply, hiccupping, that it was his job: "Who's been drinking? Me . . . Me, I never drink. I simply taste my product. That's all!"

The news of Pa's death had soon spread around the town. Ma had made a huge song and dance. We hung giant banners from the windows of our house and all over the neighborhood, between the electricity poles. Covering more than a kilometer they signposted a sort of "mourning trail," a bit like a sports run. And the day of the funeral, the hearse had driven slowly along it. Walking behind, the family, friends and local people had carried giant portraits of Pa and wreaths of artificial flowers. A traditional band had accompanied the procession, of course, because here everything needs music. And noise! No one ever complains about it. Even though the town hall hadn't given us permission to close off the public thoroughfare, a street had been covered over and white plastic chairs set up. Cars hooted as they drove around us, but that was all. They weren't going to give a widow grief, were they?

For the drinks, we had no need to worry: the SABC management provided the beer. They also handed us a fat envelope to pay for the ceremonies.

Four enormous cows from the north had been slaughtered. Then ten fat sows from Fokoué. Twenty or so goats and sheep had been butchered by old Nkono, Ma's uncle. I remember the blood spurting all over our yard, seeping into the ground, soaking into the muddy earth. Old Nkono had gazed up to the heavens: "Oh you who have departed! You our *bassogol sogol*, our ancestors, open wide your arms to welcome your son Claude Moussima Bobé."

We distributed kilos and kilos of meat around the neighborhood. Of course, people sometimes pushed and shoved and scraped their knees grabbing an extra piece of meat or a bone: beef is expensive in Cameroon. Every family came to collect their share. The mammas cooked the meat in spicy black mbongo and tomato sauce, which they then brought to the long evenings of the wake.

Groups were formed to divide up the work. Some were tasked with cooking, others with wailing, to remind us that this was a sad occasion. A neighborhood women's group, Les Dames Voisines, and a traditional band had offered to create some ambience. And what an ambience! The musicians, with their tam-tams, balafon, nkuu and gongs played Makounè, Békèlè or Bog Bés. A funeral is also a party.

Apart from Roger, who'd run away a few days before, the other absentees were the Brothers and Sisters in Christ of the Church of the True Gospel. Oh God! What a disaster! What sabotage! They'd gone around saying that Ma had killed her husband. That she was a witch, a rebel who'd been struck down by God. Didn't the Bible require women to obey their husbands as they obey the Lord? During one of his Sunday sermons, Pastor Njoh Solo had forbidden the members of his congregation from attending Pa's funeral. "You see, my dear Brothers and Sisters in Christ, the Good Lord has punished our deaconess Ngonda Moussima for her bad behavior.

God's mighty hand will always strike those who disobey His word."

Ma had felt betrayed. At the end of her strength, she'd said: "Father, forgive them for they know not what they do." Then she'd added: "Let those bastards all rot in hell!" She felt all the more hurt for having followed the pastor's advice. Without him, she never would have kept Pa at home, she'd have taken him to hospital when he first started feeling ill. But she believed all of it. She believed in it as hard as rock. The holy oil, the holy water, the holy salt, her knees grazed from praying, her Bible . . . all weapons she used against the evil that possessed her husband, but especially her son.

I clearly remember that Tuesday evening when Pastor Njoh Solo summoned Ma after the Bible study class: "My sister, the Lord says that that if your right hand causes you to sin, then cut it off and throw it away." He went on in an even more serious voice: "God tells me that you won't progress in your faith with your son. Distance yourself from him. Do you not know that it takes only one rotten seed in a granary for the entire harvest to be destroyed? Now I, the prophet and servant of God, I say to you that your husband and your son Roger are the seeds that will rot your granary. And I mean *your entire granary*! And that is serious! You absolutely must break away from these people so you can quietly follow the path of God."

22

The walls of our room at La Savane Rose are covered in mold and the paint is flaking in places. There are missing floor tiles. Simon, appalled, crushes a cockroach. The ceiling fan makes a harsh, strident sound, like that of the filthologist bitch at Yaounde police headquarters. I'm worn out. I'm hungry, I'm thirsty, I want to have a shower, say my psalms, sleep.

Before going to bed, however, switching on the ancient TV set sitting on an old table, I tune in to the national channel. It's broadcasting a documentary about the beauty of the far north of the country with a sound track of regional folk music. It shows mountain ridges, heaps of gray stones from goodness-knows-where, parched shrubs, green, yellow and even russet bushes. The russet-colored ones look out of place. And I'm struck by the clusters of mud-brick houses with their thatched roofs and all the rural charm of a region that I know, on the contrary, to be openly hostile. Thin, bare-breasted women pound grain, singing. Everything is harmonious: their high-pitched voices, the sound of their pestles thumping the wooden mortars, thump! thump! their hands clapping twice between each downward movement . . . Children play happily in the dirt nearby. They put any old thing in their mouths, perhaps a grain that's flown out of the mortar or the occasional earthworm that's escaped the hens' notice.

The program continues with images of the emissaries of our Papa-President. They bring gifts for the needy communities: sacks of rice, groundnut oil, sugar, salt, cereals and lots of other foodstuffs. An old woman pulls her scarf over her head and brushes away the flies buzzing around her with her gnarled hands. She thanks a Papa-Presidential envoy, stuffed into his three-piece suit, and his entire besuited delegation.

"What water are they supposed to cook that rice in?" fumes Simon, then starts talking about brainwashing, a shit show, propaganda . . . "Do they think we're stupid or what?!" I think he's being harsh. After all, those gifts will improve the villagers' lives, if only slightly. Simon shakes his head: "The annoying thing is that a lot of people think like you," he says. "You see things on TV, and you believe them."

"Don't you believe what you see on Facebook, too?"

"But it's not the same, Johnny! On social media, it's the witnesses talking directly . . . Look, how come we're here? What's the purpose of our trip? Solely to find Roger? But Roger's not the only one who wants boza. Can someone explain to us why people are so desperate to *go*. What are they running away from? Since we left Douala, you've seen with your own eyes how beautiful the country is, how rich. We have everything here, and I mean *everything*, but even so, people prefer to *go*, even if they have to die on the way, even if they're going to be treated like animals over there, all they want is to *go*. Why? Can you tell me?"

I turn off the TV. We are quiet for some time.

Simon gets undressed. I swear he's stark naked. Stark naked in front of me. *Our Father who art in Heaven!* I try to concentrate on saying my prayers and not stare too much at his plantain . . . *Give us this day our daily bread* . . . Daily bread my ass! This is torture! I cross my feet. I must be red all over, from head to toe, for certain. As tomato-red as a black guy can be when someone puts such a beautiful plantain and lovely athletic bum in front of his eyes. Oh Yésu! But Simon probably has no idea. He carries on talking, railing, criticizing our Papa-President's good works and criticizing some more. As for me, all I'm aware of is the horrendous throbbing in my chest, and especially down there, in my trousers. I'm going to burst. I beg for God's forgiveness, and hell! *Thank God!* I'm so relieved when Simon goes into the shower and I find myself alone. Oh Simon . . .

Beedi and Bonamoussadi are in the same *district*, the fifth. But unlike Bonamoussadi, Beedi is a very working-class area. The road surfaces are in poor condition and the pavements are dusty and have foul-smelling drains running along them.

The bars and Pentecostal churches stand side by side, taunt one another and sometimes overlap. Businesses of all kinds line the main road: hair salons for men, women and children; garages and dealers in stolen parts; untrained seamstresses; traditional healers with magic potions; and a host of shops selling single cigarettes, matches, candles or pink and yellow mint sweets. The kids call them alcohol sweets.

In the dry season, a vast shroud of dust envelops the neighborhood. The air is hot and suffocating. After three paces, you're sweating buckets. And then, in the rainy season, the slum areas (nicknamed the sôlô-quarters) are flooded. Cooking utensils and school textbooks float in the filthy water like swamp waterlilies. The mothers rush to save Sunday best outfits: because you have to give thanks to God whatever happens. Most importantly, parents carry their TV sets on their heads. No way will they miss a single Champions League match or an episode of the Mexican telenovela *The Triumph of Love*, where Victoria Ruffo plays a mother desperately searching for her daughter, Maria Desamparada.

That is the Beedi where I grew up in the early 2000s. In those days, Simon was our neighbor. He lived with his mother and his sister, Kotto, in the little clapboard house behind ours. That was long before Sita Bwanga built her White House in Ngodi-Akwa.

Several times a week, before cockcrow, Simon would come and knock at the window of the bedroom I shared with my brother; we slept on the same rubber mattress on the floor. Whereas Roger carried on snoring, I would pick up my aluminium basin and join Simon. Together, we'd walk through the alleys of the sôlô-quarters to the Ngon-èh Pond. That was where we and the other children filled our containers. Simon helped me balance my basin on my head. Once loaded, we picked our way carefully up the slippery slopes back to our respective houses. We had to make at least three or four return trips to fill the rusty barrel that stood outside each of our homes.

Half the time, our taps were dry. In any case, we drank neither the Lipton-water from the tap nor the dysentery-infested water from the Ngon-èh Pond. We drank the borehole water that my father used for making beer at the SABC. He drew it from fifty-liter jerricans that he flung into the boot of his ancient Peugeot 504. He always provided one or two for our neighbor Sita Bwanga. Simon came to fetch these supplies. When there was a shortage of drinking water, my father would proudly say: "Don't let anyone tell you otherwise, boys. The cleanest water in the world is beer!" Unbeknown to our mothers, Roger, Simon and I were then allowed to drink a few glasses of good brew.

Simon never drank himself into a stupor, which meant Pa admired him. What a kid, that Simon! At a certain point, he'd say: "I have to go and do my homework," or, "Okay, I'm going to bed. I have to be on time for school tomorrow."

All three of us went to the Conquête du Savoir High School. Punctuality was essential, especially on Monday mornings. In those days, all the students congregated in the playground: a vast concrete yard between two big gray buildings. The principal, a skinny man with a hunched back, stood in the center of these austere surroundings, not far from the mast flying our national flag. On either side of the space reserved for the principal, we formed two blocks made up of serried rows. We looked like soldiers ready for a military parade.

Simon found himself opposite me, at the head of the facing row. A permanent smile on his lips. But on those mornings, I knew that that smile was for me, *only for me*, because he punctuated it with a friendly, brotherly wink. Slightly teasing. I'd give him a discreet smile in acknowledgment. Then we'd resume the earnest expression required of us. We sang the national anthem at the tops of our voices, arms by our sides. Then, we listened as the principal barked the weekly speech that we knew by heart: "My friends, fortune only favors those who work hard. Neither God nor any marabout will do anything that your brain can't do itself. Work hard and dress smartly. The rest will follow."

Simon was always neatly turned-out: shoes carefully polished, khaki trousers with impeccable creases, a sky-blue, short-sleeved shirt with four front pockets. The one on the top right bore the school's coat of arms. His mother had embroidered his name in red: Moudjonguè Simon. He's always known how to look after himself: he wore his hair short, his nails well trimmed. His face smooth. The day before, he took the time to shave his beard, because, yes, he already had one back then. Which in my eyes made him appear more adult, reassuring. He lathered his stubbly chin until a foam formed. With his left hand, he held a shard of mirror and in the other, his disposable Bic razor. He twisted his neck every which way to seek out and remove every single hair. When he shaved, I watched him, fascinated, wondering whether I'd have a beard one day. (Even Roger, at fourteen, didn't have one yet.)

Sometimes, during the week, Simon would ask me to give him a dictation. While I read him excerpts from one of the few books available to us, Roger would make fun of the way I enunciated each syllable. He said that by reading like that, I was helping Simon make as few mistakes as possible. "At school, friends do everything they can to cause the others to make mistakes," he added.

Simon and Roger were in the same class in the fourth year. They were working toward their national school certificate exam. The test they most dreaded was dictation. That was why the teaching staff gave them a dictation every day. Each student in turn had to read a passage of their choice. One spelling mistake, one mark deducted. Two for a grammatical error, and half a mark for accents, cedillas or apostrophes. Simon told me that his classmates were even stricter than their teachers. They turned into real sleuths, sniffing out the slightest error. At the end, if your mark was below 15/20, you had to write out the text five times – without making any further mistakes, of course. And if a student was unlucky enough for a teacher to spot another mistake during their hasty check, they were beaten.

Spare the rod, spoil the child.

Like me, Simon was afraid of the whip. Before our dictation sessions, he'd often whisper: "I don't want to get a beating, do I, Johnny!" He hated them, not only because of the physical pain they caused, but also, and most of all, because of the shame. He thought it unfair that Ma should beat Roger so much because he went out partying for a short time. Wednesday afternoon kids' matinees weren't really his thing. He preferred to spend time with me, reading, doing homework or watching TV. He told me one evening he'd been whipped in front of his classmates because he hadn't done his math homework. He'd simply forgotten. He, Simon, the model student, had experienced the mother of all humiliations! Hence his aversion to the whip. He'd never have admitted that to his classmates, no, and especially not to Roger, who'd have called him a scaredy-cat, a sissy.

Simon almost never had less than 15/20. As we left school for the day, I'd often ask him: "So, how did your dictation go today?"

"Well easy!" he'd reply triumphantly. "No mistakes!"

"How about Roger?"

"Meh!" he'd sigh with a shrug. "I think he's going to have to write it out five times."

On the way home, Simon explained loads of things that I hadn't understood in class. Pythagoras's theorem for example. He'd say: "You see Jean, it's very easy. Open your ears wide and listen to me: in a right-angled triangle, the square of the length of the hypotenuse is equal to the sum of squares of the lengths of other two sides. D'you get it?" I'd frown. He formulated it and reformulated several times so that I could, in turn, repeat the rule clearly. But I couldn't grasp it. At least, not like him. I thought of Roger. Simon and I knew very well that he wasn't copying out his text. He opted for football training instead. The spanking? Oh, he didn't give a toss about that! It was as if the thrashings he received at home had toughened him up.

23

Simon had fallen asleep in the bed, stark naked.

And lead us not into temptation ... but the damage was already done, I had already committed the abomination. Thinking about him, I'd jerked off twice in the shower. In fact, I wonder whether he'd heard me come, I'd found it so hard to stifle my moans.

As I'm leaving the room to go and get something to eat, my phone rings: it's Ma. She's glad to hear my voice. I tell her we've arrived safely in Garoua. She shouts her surprise, her delight. She's never been that far. She only knows Douala and Yaounde. I tell her that tomorrow we'll be taking the first bush taxi for Maroua. No, she needn't worry, we still have enough money left.

A long silence. "Hello? Are you there?" She's there, but she's crying, and her sobs hit me like missiles. "Is everything okay?" A brief silence. I ask her again. She says that everything will be all right, "by the grace of God." She immediately adds, her voice hoarse and phlegmy: "Claude was a bastard, you understand, my Choupi! A complete fool. I wonder how I could even have spent my life with a bastard like that. A fat pig! I pray to God that your brother doesn't turn out like him." Another great sob, and then she hangs up without even a little "Ciao!" Oh God! Of course I'm worried. Since Pa's death, she's done nothing but cry. She threatens she'll beat him and bite him when they come face-to-face with each other, up there, with Yésu. But this evening, it's different: there's a blind fury in her voice. I wake Simon and tell him about it. Staring at the ceiling, he utters a deep sigh but says nothing. I try to call Ma back to find out what's going on: "I'm sorry I can't take your call right now, please leave a message." Maybe we should phone Sita Bwanga. I can go back straight away if I have to. I can . . . "Hey Simon! Have you lost your tongue?"

"No," says Simon, calmly. "It'll be fine. Your mother just needs some rest."

"What? But even so, it's weird, isn't it? What can be the matter *this time*?"

"Calm down, okay Johnny?"

He put his arms around me. Nooo! Please don't do that. Oh Simon! Don't you realize you're butt naked? As if he hears my desperate plea, he puts on a pair of shorts and assumes the solemn expression I know so well. "Come and sit here. Come on, come here."

Simon's going to tell me something. My heart's pounding as if it will burst. Is he going to tell me (at last!) that *we're two of a kind*? No. The mother of all disappointments! He says this is a story Sita Bwanga told him not so long ago – a few days after Roger ran away. He makes me promise to keep my mouth shut as tight as a smoked fish. "*I swear!*"

He explains that it goes back to one terrible Friday in 1989, on the eve of the summer holidays. Ma was only sixteen. On coming home from the Lycée Joss, where she was studying for her school certificate, she found her mother sitting on a little wooden bench in front of their house in Deïdo. Mbôbo Yayi was slicing cassava for the evening meal. Ma offered to help, but Mbôbo Yayi was lost in her thoughts and didn't answer her. So Ngonda went and sat next to her, to cut up the cassava: slice off the top and bottom of the long tuber, then chop it into two or three pieces and peel them meticulously, trying not to waste any of the precious starch.

"The Moussima Bobé family wants to *take you in*," Mbôbo Yayi had eventually said.

"*Take me in?* What do you mean?"

"They say you'd be good for their son Claude."

"Claude Moussima Bobé?"

"You know, he's working in Yaounde now, at the SABC, and he'll soon be transferred here, to Douala. He's a well-mannered young man and his family is respectable."

"Yes, but can you eat respect?" Ma asked.

"Oh, Ngonda!"

"Ma, I no longer understand this family. One day you say that the Moussima Bobés are our relatives, then another day you say I have to marry one of their sons. Does a girl marry her brother? Well, does she?"

Mbôbo Yayi carried on peeling the cassava in silence, says Simon, who goes on:

"'Okay,' your mother added. 'If you think it's good for me, I agree. But that son of theirs can wait until I've finished school, can't he? You know, I'm sitting the typing baccalaureate to become a secretary.'

"'You've spoken well, daughter. I'll talk to your father. I think the Moussima Bobés will agree. We're leaving next week to spend the holidays in the village.'

"On their arrival at Pout-Loloma, they found the place buzzing. There was talk of nothing but the dancing, the prelude to the traditional Elog Mpoo festival that's due to take place a few months later, in honor of the illustrious Bassa family.

"Your mother brought out her fuchsia dress with very wide shoulder pads. A wide imitation-leather belt cinched her waist. And to differentiate herself from the village girls, she wore clip-on earrings, big, golden ones in the shape of a starfish." (I remember having seen those earrings myself in a photo of Ma when she was young. Wearing lipstick and rouge, she looked classy in her little patent-leather court shoes decorated with bows.) "Whereas she'd often thought that her lycée's very short, regulation hairstyle was unflattering, on that day, she realized that her tomboy look actually emphasized her femininity.

"They sang along to all the hit tunes at the tops of their voices, even when they didn't know the words. Songs like *Ma Ding Ma Wog* by Maele from Equatorial Guinea.

"Your mother danced, danced, daaaaanced to that music. Then someone grabbed her around the waist.

"'Oh Claude, what are you doing here?'

"'I'm having fun, like you, my darling.'

"'Me, your darling? Since when?'

"All the same, she graciously accepted the next dance, captivated by Grace Decca's rich voice. Spontaneously – and naively – she put her arms around your father's neck and he even planted a little kiss on her forehead at the end of the dance. And then, laughing, she went out into the bush and started running. But Claude caught up with her.

"I'm repeating word for word the conversation as told to me by my mother the other day:

"'Hey, darling, where are you running off to like that?'

"'Oh Claude! I need a pee. I have to hurry or I'll wet myself.'

"'And you're going to your place for a little wee? Do it here, in the forest. No one can see you.'

"'Are you calling yourself no one?'

"'Are you afraid of me, my sweetheart?'

"'*I beg*, Claude, let me go home. Besides, people say there are evil snakes in this forest. *Better* I . . .'

"'Go on! . . . I'm here. No need to *tremble* like that, my love, is there?'

"In the end, Ngonda gave in. She shyly took her clothes off, behind a bush. Claude moved close to her to shield her from view. Shield her? Yeah, right! Ha ha. She'd barely put her underwear back on when he'd pulled his down and whipped out his plantain, which was hard. Oh Yésu! that terrified your mother. Claude no longer bore any resemblance to the charming man she'd just danced with. This man she wanted to hit and bite, she wanted to smash his head in with a *mbobotò*, a large stone.

"'But Claude, we're not married,' she gasped, her heart almost still.

"'Married or not, it doesn't matter, my darling.'

"'Oh yes it does. I don't want to. And I don't even know about these things.'

"'But darling, it's better that way.'

"She implored him to wait. He mustn't do that to her. And where? In the middle of the bush! That was the worst thing for her, coming from the city. No, he should just wait a little longer! In a few months, in a few years, she'd be more devoted and obedient than he could dream of, that was for certain. She promised him: she would be the smoothly ground groundnut in his ndoleh, she would be the sugar in his tapioca, she would even be, yes, the *piment* that he'd crush every night as he pleased. All that only for him. But for that, he would have to wait. Now everything that your mother came out with that day, the nonsense and enticements to stop him from doing it, on the contrary, aroused Claude a hundred times more. He was convinced she liked that, the tease, the little minx – and that she wanted it as much as he did, wanted his plantain and his juice.

"That's how your mother became pregnant with Roger."

24

Leaving La Savane Rose, I notice a young woman whose face is half hidden behind a pagne she's wearing as a veil. She bangs on the door of one of the rooms. A man's voice answers: "One moment, I'm coming!" and when she sees me, she immediately lowers her gaze. I see a similar scene in front of another door, with another pimentière. I hope the man at reception has a metal detector to control the comings and goings of all these girls.

I wander through the streets of Garoua. It's much quieter than Douala or Yaounde. On my left is the Boulangerie du Marché. It's probably too expensive. I make do with the roadside vendors, buying a hunk of bread with suya from one of them. I've barely bitten into it when a kid appears, pleading with his eyes. His already bald head is covered in ringworm, his ragged clothes stink. At first, I recoil. Then I give him my bread and two coins. He smiles at me and skips off.

I think about Ma. Why didn't she say anything to me, her Choupi? How shameful to learn this from Simon's lips. It's true, he's also my brother, yes, but . . . but he shouldn't be the one to tell me such a terrible thing. And does Roger know this whole story? Oh God!

After what he did to her, it's amazing that Ma still lived with Pa all those years. She probably felt a tiny bit of love for him. A tiny bit. Well, love, or desire. Because if she didn't, she wouldn't have given him another child. Unless I'm not Pa's son. Who knows? Maybe in those days in Pout-Loloma, people already did what the village chiefs do in the north do to girls who are raped by Boko Haram: hand them over to their attackers . . .

Even though I'm the spitting image of Ngonda, I do have something of my father. Let's have a look: my nose is more or less like his. Not as flat, but still. As children, we enjoyed seeking out resemblances to our parents. Roger would tell me that my fingers were as long and tapering as Pa's. That similarity was hard to see, but eventually, I ended up believing it. Yes, yes, it's true: my fingers are just like Pa's . . . and Ma's: hers are just as long and tapering . . . In short, why scratch my ass with all these pointless thoughts. It's not important! What's certain is that Ma didn't do an *Agatha Moudio;* I'm as black as my *father.*

Besides, Ma had me at a time when she was already a fanatical follower of the Church of the True Gospel. She would never have permitted herself to have an affair. Those who were unfaithful to their husbands, or suspected of wanting to be, were excommunicated on the spot. But I have to admit that each time I saw the son of Sister Roberta, I was struck by his resemblance to Pastor Njoh Solo. One day I said as much to Ma. "You mustn't blaspheme, my Choupi."

Let's not give it any more thought. I'm clinging to the hope of finding Roger the next day at El Hadj Bassirou's place. What will I say to him? I haven't the slightest idea. In any case, I won't tell him Ma's *story*. Perhaps I'll just ask him to come back home. Or I'll convince him that Ma's truly sorry for the suffering she's caused him. Without really knowing if that's actually true. Because that's how Ma is, she never says sorry. She refuses to be wrong. According to her, a mother must always be right. She's the God of her children on earth.

One evening, after school, I'd found Ngonda at home, sitting in the Chief's chair. She was with Roger and two gentlemen. I already knew the younger one. He'd spotted my brother during his first match with the Nyanga Boys of Bonamoussadi. I found out later that the other gentleman was called Ayissi and that he wanted to manage Roger's football future.

"Monsieur Ayissi," began Ma in a calm but firm voice. "For the love of God, leave my son alone. He's only seventeen. Instead of advising him to study, you're cramming his big head with football. Is football a living? Is it?"

"Madame . . ."

"I asked you if playing football is a living. Is it a real job? We all want a good future for our sons: for them to get up in the morning, put on their suit and tie, pick up their briefcase and go to work. That's a real-real job. Do you understand?"

"Madame," interrupted the agent, "you know a person can earn a very good living playing football. For example, look at . . ."

"Who switched him on?" Ma retorted impulsively. "Was I speaking to you? If a person could earn a living from football, then you wouldn't be sitting here in my armchair, all unkempt like the only survivor of a family of sell-outs. And anyway, who are you in this business?"

"He's the agent, Bernard Donkeu," replied Roger.

"Donkeu?! That's all we need, a Bamileke mixed up in this."

I've never understood what Ma has against the Bamileke. I've rarely heard her speak well of them. She says they're traitors, dishonest and underhand, who make money out of others. She often adds that if she does deal with them, it's because they have a stranglehold on the country's economy. She says: "They're our Jews." When she used to say things like that at home, Pa would get annoyed: "Oh Ngonda, tribalism isn't Christian, is it?" Ma would reply that if God hadn't been a bit tribalistic Himself, he'd never have singled out and chosen only one people on Earth.

"We're here to talk about your son's talent, and not the Bamileke," said Monsieur Ayissi, perspiring with embarrassment and trying to steer the conversation back on track.

"Oh, are you? You come to my house to attack me and call me tribalistic, and I'm supposed to let you get away with it. Is that it?"

"No one has attacked you, Madame . . ."

"And now you're calling me a liar."

"But Madame . . ."

"Out!"

"Ma, please," Roger broke in.

"You be quiet when I'm speaking. Gentle Jesus! So you think it's fine to bring these lowlifes into my house to disrespect me . . . Oh Roger! What am I going to do with you? Tell me what I can do to teach you? Right, I'm going to count to three and if these rogues aren't gone, the hand of God Himself will strike them."

The agent Bernard Donkeu and the manager Ayissi stood up. Then Ayissi asked: "Could we at least have a word with your husband?"

"My husband?" laughed Ma. "My word outweighs my husband's. There's no point trying to take shortcuts behind my back. No means no, okay? You make sure that Roger goes to school. Look at my Choupi, eh, look at him . . . he's the youngest by two years and he'll be sitting his baccalaureate soon. Aren't you ashamed, Roger? And you good-for-nothings, you *rientons*, you're encouraging him to be foolish."

"But Madame . . ."

"Get out of my house! Otherwise there'll be trouble."

"Madame . . ."

"Out, I said!"

Roger tried to talk to Pa about it, tried to persuade him. In vain. Pa told him he couldn't challenge so final a decision by his wife. For once, he agreed with her. He criticized Roger for falling behind in his studies. Once again, he compared him with me.

25

On either side of the asphalt road, the savannah stretches as far as the eye can see. In the distance, we glimpse a herd of thin cows with long horns. A young cowherd brandishing a stick is doing his best to guide them. As we draw closer, the bus driver slows down. The animals move out of the way in their own good time, in no hurry. Their way of grazing is so unsteady that they look as if they're perched on stiletto heels.

On the road, police searches are more and more frequent. Each time, it's the same song and dance: get out of the vehicle, present your ID, be frisked by officers with metal detectors, then get back in a few meters further on. There is an even stronger police presence on the road between Garoua and Maroua. Meanwhile, the view through the windows is utterly breathtaking! For the past two hours, it's crazy! But when I remind myself that behind that glorious vegetation, those mounds of stones and caramel-colored mountains conceal pockets of Allah fanatics, the beauty of the landscape is a lot less appealing.

At the Sahel Voyage bus station in Maroua, Simon anxiously checks his phone but there's no signal – 4G hasn't yet reached this area. So he won't be able to contact the White Queen on Facebook – shit! – or call the Gazelle of Melen. Which I'm glad about.

It's extremely hot. Simon is shivering and sweating profusely. He sponges himself with his T-shirt. When I ask if he's okay, he yells at me: "Leave me alone, for fuck's sake!" Then he walks off, comes back and says in a fury: "You've done fuck all since the start of this trip. You're doing fuck all! Even after what I told you yesterday, you're making no effort. *None!* You're there sniveling like a kid, you're such a faggot! Roger was right, you really are your mother's little baby! It makes you wonder whether it's your brother we're looking for or mine?"

Simon's words strike me like an arrow. Coming from his lips, they hurt even more than Roger's blows.

Dejected, I sit down on a little rock in front of the Sahel Voyage ticket window. As a woman unknots her pagne to pay for her ticket, she drops some money without realizing. I'm about to tell her when a little boy picks up the note and gives it back to the lady. She smiles and thanks him in a language I don't understand. She even gives him a coin, and I watch the kid walk off, happy. If someone had told me that that could happen in Cameroon, I'd never have believed it: perhaps because, until then, my Cameroon had been limited to Douala.

I catch up with the boy and tell him I'm looking for a friend. He immediately frowns. Does he even speak French? Then I try and make myself understood with gestures, and he replies in a high-pitched voice: "*Walahi Bilahi*, brother! There are a lot of Papas here in Djoudandou. Which Papa are you looking for exactly?" I sigh. What an idiot I was to think he didn't speak French. "Monsieur Bassirou. El Hadj Bassirou," I reply. The kid gives me a big smile.

"Alhadji Bassirou?"

"No, El Hadj Bassirou."

"It's the same thing, brother."

"Are you sure?"

"Walahi Bilahi, it's the same thing! That's what we call someone who's already been to the home of Allah, in Mecca."

"Okay. Then I'm looking for Alhadji Bassirou."

"Everyone here in Djoudandou knows Alhadji Bassirou!"

The kid gazes at me. "*Are you also looking for the road?*" No, no, no. I'm looking for someone. My brother.

Can he help me? It's not clear. He says he still has to carry many-many suitcases if he wants to bring a few cents home to his *daada*. Simon joins us, still just as edgy. I explain the situation and he gives a large-denomination note to little Yaya. It's well deserved. I'm certain this little kid's not going to screw us. "Come on Yaya, let's go!"

Since we won't let him carry our bags, Yaya capers ahead like a mountain goat. Following behind, we walk through narrow, sandy streets where, miraculously, dry shrubs with green leaves grow. A few vendors wearing gandouras wait beneath multicolored umbrellas for unlikely customers. Again, and always, that smell of adulterated petrol, the headache-inducing throbbing of the motorcycle taxis, the shrill laughter of women with calabashes on their heads, a perspiring rickshaw driver, kids chasing after a rusty bicycle wheel rim. This desert neighborhood is relatively calm, apart from two soldiers, fingers on triggers, expressions blank, standing beside their dark-blue pickup.

Yaya points to a group of men and says: "You see over there, those are the *baapa*, the tontons. They're on the watchdog committee. Because Boko Haram is killing everywhere now, our baapa keep watch over the neighborhood, the mosques and the markets. When they see strange-strange people like the burqa-girls, wham bam! they arrest them and call the military. The commando brigades arrive, pow-pow! Pow-pow! If they're Boko Haram girls, aaah! the commandos arrest them, throw them into prison and give the tontons a medal to say *ossoko*, thank you. But often, the tontons are unlucky, eh Allah! It turns out it's just a little girl who was innocently on her way to the market to buy some millet for her daada. Then the commandos let her go. Me, when I'm grown up, I'm going to be a soldier and I'll throw all the little burqa-girls in prison, because *Wilahi Bilahi!* you never know with those girls. You have to be very-very careful with them!"

It so happens that a tonton steps away from the group and comes over to us. He's wearing simple flip-flops and a faded boubou on which three medals are prominently displayed. He has a gun slung over his shoulder as if it's the latest Kalashnikov. First he greets young Yaya: "*Saanou! Jam'na?*" They exchange a few words in their language – I later discover that it's Fula – then the tonton turns to us:

"Greetings, my brothers. I'm Alidou Chabib. I am head of the anti-Boko Haram watchdog committee here in Djoudandou. Yaya has explained everything to me, but first I must check your bags." We let him, without a word. Alidou Chabib doesn't have the famous metal detector. He prods and pokes our bags, hands them back and says: "Allah protect you. I hope you find your brother. Good luck!" We in turn wish him all the best for his mission, and above all, many medals.

A few minutes later, Yaya stops: "You see over there?" he says, "the house down there opposite the mosque. That's Alhadji Bassirou's place." Simon gives him a final tip. Yaya thanks him. "I have to go back to the bus station," he says. "I've got a lot more work today. Good luck!" He waves goodbye and he's off.

At Alhadji Bassirou's house, a young woman opens the door to us. A voluptuous, smiling woman with a round face. She shows us onto the dusty terrace and invites us to sit down on two low stools. She points to Alhadji Bassirou's back – he's in the middle of a prayer session. Under his voluminous white gandoura, I notice, as well as his paunch, that his skin that is as light and copper-colored as Kotto's.

A few minutes later, he tells his beads in front of us. A pom-pom dangles from the end of the string of beads. "*Assalam' Alaykum!*" he says, shaking each of our hands in turn. Is he really the spiritual son of Benghazi Omar?

This religious man can't have drunk a drop of alcohol ever. Especially not in bars until late into the night. It's hard to picture him in hotspots like Mini Ferme Melen, with its trannies, whores and low life. Besides, he's a lot older than Omar. His red chechia does not conceal his graying frizzy hair. There are two deep wrinkles on his forehead, which has a huge black birthmark – he's a *real* Muslim.

He sits on a mat facing us and pours us Arab-style mint tea from a height, rhythmically raising and lowering his arm. The young woman brings us bissap. I drain my glass in one gulp, I was so thirsty. Oddly, I feel very much at home here. As for Simon, he hasn't touched his glass. He watches Alhadji Bassirou very warily. "Hazim and the others left for Mokolo the night before last," Alhadji Bassirou tells us, without our having opened our mouths. He goes on: "I heard this morning that they managed to cross the border into Nigeria. Allah be praised. They will arrive in Maiduguri perhaps this evening, if all goes well."

Simon and I wonder who Hazim is. Alhadji Bassirou takes another sip of tea then continues: "He is no longer called Roger, or Joker. All that's over. That's the past. His name is now Hazim Mouzzafar. *Barak'Allah!* May the Lord be blessed! A new soul has been given to him. Hazim recited the *Shahada* and placed himself in the service of the Almighty."

Alhadji Bassirou knows about our journey. He has prayed for us a lot and gives thanks to God for having protected us. He tried to delay Hazim's departure for as long as possible, by one or two days, but he was unable to do more. Hazim Mouzzafar had been determined to leave. And the others weren't prepared to wait a hundred and seven years for his brothers.

"In any case, I very quickly realized that your presence wasn't going to make any difference. Hazim knew you were on the way here. He could have waited for you, but that wasn't what he wanted to do. This country isn't made for him. Football here isn't played the way he wants to play. Do you understand? His parents, you, the pain he's caused you . . . he's put everything into the hands of Allah. He alone, the Almighty, will render justice on Judgment Day. What more could I do than give him my blessing? *Insh'Allah*, may he be successful!"

To my great surprise, this revelation devastates Simon. He starts sobbing like a baby. I've never seen him like this. Alhadji Bassirou puts his arms around him. But Simon is inconsolable. Oh Lord! What's happened to my tough Simon? Tough my ass, yeah! He's just his mother Bwanga's precious little Choupi! The guy who hangs out with blond trannies and ugly fanta-coka girls. That's the brave guy he is. So cry away, you little softie! Eeesh!

I ask for another glass of bissap, down it in one and go for a little walk, on my own, outside. Oh, I have so many things to tell Ma! "Hello, Ma?"

"Yes, my Choupi. Tell me. Where are you? Have you found him?

ACKNOWLEDGMENTS

The author wishes to thank Amaury Nauroy for his support.

Ros Schwartz wishes to thank Félicité, Hector, Diane, Rolland, James, Njamsi and N'for, participants in the translation workshop hosted by Bakwa publishers in October 2019, for their invaluable suggestions, and also chef Théo Akira Moyo Diefe for making the dishes mentioned in this book.

Glossary

asso: customer

bassogol sogol: ancestors

bissap: hibiscus tea

bobolo: precooked cassava stick wrapped in leaves

boza: expression used by Central and West African migrants attempting to reach Europe when they manage to cross the border. Meaning "victory," the term is thought to come from Wolof or Bambara.

bozayer: person attempting *boza*

daada: Fulani for *mother*

feyman: swindler

gandoura: a kind of light tunic, in wool or cotton, with or without sleeves. It is worn primarily in the Middle East and North Africa.

gaou: a wimp, a loser (similar to a *mougou*, see below)

impeubable: untouchable, in the sense that no one can do anything to a person

joor: a word used for emphasis

kaba ngondo : a voluminous ankle-length dress with wide sleeves

kai wallai: watch out

kongossa: gossip

Mbeng: France

mbéré: a cop

mbongo: black powdered burnt spice used to make a sauce of the same name. A speciality of the Bassa people

mboundja: shoot!

mintoumba: fermented cassava bread with red palm oil

mola: guy

mougou: a wimp

ndoleh: dish consisting of stewed nuts, bitter leaves indigenous to West Africa and fish or beef

nga: a woman

nguigna: strength

na how? hello, how goes it?

nsanga: a mixture of maize, cassava leaf and palm nut juice

pagne: a long, rectangular, often brightly colored or decorated piece of cloth that is wrapped tightly about the torso with the ends usually falling free or that is used as a loincloth or undergarment

panthère: seductive, scantily dressed young woman

plantain: here a euphemism for penis

piment/pimentière: literally chili pepper/chili pepper-vendor, meaning sex/prostitute in Camfranglais

sôlô-quarter: slum neighborhood

suya: spicy meat skewer

tourne-dos: roadside restaurant where customers eat with their backs turned to the road

touma: pass the ball

Walahi Bilahi: walahi means I swear to God, in Arabic, while *bilahi* is just a word that rhymes *wanda:* to be surprised

zero macabo: schoolchildren's song taunting those with poor exam results

zoua-zoua : adulterated petrol

Max Lobe was born in Douala, Cameroon. At eighteen he moved to Switzerland, where he earned a BA in communication and journalism and a master's in public policy and administration. In 2017, his novel *Confidences* won the Ahmadou Kourouma Prize. *A Long Way from Douala*, his latest novel, was published in 2018 to rave reviews in Switzerland and France. Other books include *39 rue de Berne* and *La Trinité bantoue*. Max Lobe lives in Geneva.

Ros Schwartz is an award-winning translator of more than 100 works of fiction and non fiction, including the 2010 edition of Antoine de Saint-Exupéry's *The Little Prince*. Among the Francophone authors she has translated are Tahar Ben Jelloun, Aziz Chouaki, Fatou Diome, Dominique Eddé and Ousmane Sembène. In 2009, she was made a Chevalier de l'Ordre des Arts et des Lettres, and in 2017 she was awarded the John Sykes Memorial Prize for Excellence.